# DEDICATION

*A Time Like This is dedicated to my husband, Rick, who is always there for me - in good times and bad. Thank you "Boog" for all the support and encouragement you give me.*

A Time Like This

ISBN 978-0-9969447-2-4

# TABLE OF CONTENTS

# LIST OF CHARACTERS

1. Aaron (*Air-un*): Zechariah's eldest son
2. Amitis (*Au-me-tees*): Sura's mother-in-law
3. Armand (*Are-mund*): King Xerxes' eunuch
4. Artunis (*Are-toon-iss*): Servant girl
5. Babak (*Bah-back*): Sura's eldest grandson
6. Benjamin (*Ben-juh-men*): Zechariah's younger son
7. Binu (*Buh-new*): Sura's brother
8. Chista (*Kissed-a*): Sura's best friend
9. Daniel (*Dan-yell*): Youngest son of Maai
10. Dinah (*Die-nuh*): Binu's wife
11. Eli (*Ee-lie*): Binu's son
12. Eliashib (*El-ia-shib*) Priest friend of Tobiah
13. Farhad (*Far-hod*): Sura's husband
14. Geshem (*Guessh-em*): Enemy of Nehemiah
15. Haman (*Hay-mun*): King Xerxes' head prince
16. Hannah (*Han-nuh*): Aaron's wife
17. Hegai (*Hig-eye*): Esther's eunuch
18. Jacob (*Jay-cub*): Benjamin's son
19. King Artaxerxes (*Art-uh-Zerk-cees*): King Xerxes' son
20. King Xerxes (*Zerk-cees*): King of Persia (486-464 B.C.)
21. Maai (*May-eye*): Zechariah's elderly neighbor
22. Mandana (*Mahn-don-ah*): Concubine
23. Memucan (*Meh-muh-kun*): King Xerxes' prince

24. Meres (*Mare-ess*): King Xerxes' prince

25. Mica (*My-kah*): Son of Maai

26. Miriam (*Mere-ee-um*): Benjamin's wife

27. Mordecai (*More-dah-kay-eye*): Queen Esther's cousin

28. Narses (*Nar-sis*): Sura's youngest grandson

29. Nehemiah (*Nee-huh-my-ah*): Governor of Jerusalem

30. Otanes (*O-tanes*): Sura's son

31. Queen Esther, aka Hadassah (*Huh-das-uh*): Second wife of Xerxes

32 Queen Vashti (*Vash-tee*): First wife of Xerxes

33. Rachel (*Ray-chel*): Eli's wife

34. Rebekah (*Ruh-beck-uh*): Zechariah's wife

35. Ruth *(Rooth)*: Eli's baby daughter

36. Sanballat (*San-buh-let*): Enemy of Nehemiah

37. Shemaiah (*She-my-uh*): Hired enemy of Nehemiah

38. Shemmah (*She-maw*): Sura's granddaughter

39. Shirin (*She-reen*): Otanes' wife

40. Sura (*Soo-ruh*): Servant / Main character

41. Tobiah (*Tow-by-ah*): Enemy of Nehemiah

42. Yousef (*Yoo-seff*): King Xerxes' scribe

43. Zechariah (*Zeck-uh-rye-uh*): Sura's oldest brother

44. Zeresh (*Zare-esh*): Haman's wife

45. Zethar (*Zeh-thar*): King Xerxes' eunuch

# A TIME LONG AGO

1

Change. You can sense when it is about to happen. Sura couldn't identify the reason for the chill down her spine, but she sensed something ominous was around the corner. This feeling of doom was in stark contrast to the beautiful colors of red, orange, and yellow in the sky as the sun began to set behind the Zagros Mountains in Persia.

The year was 444 B.C., during the reign of the King Artaxerxes. Sura sat on a large floor cushion with her eight year old granddaughter, Shemmah. Her daughter-in-law, Shirin, swept their modest hut. Sura's grandsons played sword-fight in the corner of the room with their home-made wooden swords.

Sura had been a servant to Queen Esther for many years, and most of those years had been less than kind to Sura. At an early age she was sold into slavery, became a widow soon after marriage, and had raised her son alone. She had gained her freedom, but was now losing her sight. Sura lived with her son and his family. As she sat in a dimly lit room, she heard a rattling sound at the door, which drew her attention. "What do I hear? Who are you?"

Sura's son quickly entered the room. His wife's heart still skipped a beat when she looked at him and his rugged good looks. As he placed his helmet onto the floor, he answered his mother, "Maman, it's I, Otanes."

Sura slowly stood up and walked towards his voice. "What is it, son? I can tell when you're distressed."

Otanes looked over at his wife and then to his mother, his daughter, and his sons. "There is news from the king." Otanes caught his breath. "He is sending several of us captains to Jerusalem with his cupbearer, Nehemiah, to help rebuild the wall around the city, which the Babylonians destroyed. There is much opposition to the rebuilding. There have been many threats of attacks from the Jews' enemies, so the king is sending us to maintain order."

Shirin quickly stopped sweeping. Her dark-brown eyes had a questioning look. "How long will you be gone?"

Otanes put his hand on his wife's shoulder and replied, "The king doesn't know how many years we will be there, so he has given us permission to take our families with us. We're leaving in two days. You, Maman, and the children need to prepare for the trip."

Shirin's brow wrinkled with concern. She asked, "Where will we live once we arrive in Jerusalem?"

Sura choked back tears as she tried to control her emotions. "I had relatives around Jerusalem. If they are still alive, perhaps we can stay with them."

A look of shock came across Otanes' face. He exclaimed, "Relatives around Jerusalem! This is the first time I've heard of them."

Sura wiped her eyes and sat back down onto the floor cushion. "After the Babylonian king, Nebuchadnezzar, laid siege to Jerusalem, the Jews who were not killed in the siege went into captivity. My great-grandparents, who were born in Jerusalem, were among those captured and sent to Babylon. My baba-bozorg (grandfather) was born during this time of captivity in Babylon."

Shemmah laid her head in her grandmother's lap. "How did your relatives get back to Jerusalem from Babylon?"

Otanes and Shirin sat down on their cushions, and their sons, Babak and Narses, each placed their cushions close to their grandmother. Sura stroked Shemmah's hair and continued her story.

"Many years after the reign of the Babylonian King Nebuchadnezzar, King Cyrus of the Persian Empire successfully conquered the City of Babylon. As he entered the city he was presented an ancient scroll of Isaiah that contained a personal letter addressed by name to Cyrus. Not only did it contain his name, but it also described his career and his history. Now, the prophet Isaiah had died one hundred and fifty-years before this event."

Babak, Sura's eldest grandson, looked at his grandmother with a quizzical look. "How could Isaiah know about this man one hundred and fifty-years before he was born, Maman-Bozorg (Grandmother)?"

Sura looked at her grandson as she brushed her hair out of her eyes. "With man, it's impossible; but with God, all things are possible. He knows all things before they happen."

Shemmah snuggled in Sura's lap, and Sura continued, "King Cyrus was impressed with the prediction in Isaiah calling him by name and how Isaiah also told of how Cyrus would allow the Jews to return and rebuild the temple in Jerusalem. So he wrote a decree allowing the

Jews to do that very thing. My baba-bozorg was among those who went to Jerusalem."

"What happened when they arrived in Jerusalem?" Shemmah asked while she twirled her hair with her fingers.

Sura laughed. "You are so much like me. I used to twirl my hair just like you."

Narses, Sura's youngest grandson, sat up on his cushion. "So, Maman-Bozorg, tell us, what happened? What did they do when they got to Jerusalem?"

As Sura straightened up, she answered, "Ah yes, back to my story. King Cyrus appointed a man named Zerubbabel, a leader in Jerusalem, to oversee the work on the temple. Among the almost fifty-thousand workers who worked on the temple was my baba-bozorg. Not long after the construction started, there arose opposition from their enemies. After the Jews went into exile, many people moved in and around Jerusalem. When the Jews came back from their exile, they harassed them. For fifteen years, they tried to stop the reconstruction of the temple. They did not want the Jews back in the land."

Shirin arose and brought everyone a cup, and as she was pouring saffron tea into each cup, she asked Sura, "Is this when your parents were born?"

Sura took a sip of her tea and answered, "Yes, my baba (father) and maman (mother) were born at this time, during the rule of King Darius. Tattenai, the governor of the region beyond the Euphrates, wrote a letter to the king to try and stop the construction."

Otanes placed his cup down on the low table in front of their cushions. "Then what happened?"

Sura leaned back on her elbow and continued. "King Darius ordered a search be made of the Babylonian archives. A decree was discovered written by King Cyrus allowing the temple rebuilt and all expenses paid from the royal bank. King Darius wrote to Tattenai to stay out of the way and leave Zerubbabel and the Jewish leaders alone to work on their temple."

Otanes leaned back, looking at his mother with interest. "How did you end up here in the Persian capital of Susa?"

Repositioning herself on the cushion, Sura answered with a crack in her voice, "Things were difficult for the families in Jerusalem during the reconstruction of the temple. Many families found it hard to supply enough food for themselves and all their children. My baba and maman sold me to a group of Persians who were traveling through. It was not unusual to sell their daughters and keep their sons. I had three older brothers, and I was the only daughter. I was the same age as Shemmah when I was sold into slavery."

Shemmah gave her grandmother a tearful look. "Oh Maman-Bozorg, that's awful."

Sura gave Shemmah a little smile. "It wasn't all bad. I was raised by a Persian family here in Susa. I considered them my parents and they treated me as their own."

Otanes got up from his cushion and helped his wife up. "Shirin, you, Maman, and the children don't need to worry about a thing. Thirteen years ago Ezra, the priest, led many Jews back to Jerusalem. They made repairs to some of the abandoned residences in and around Jerusalem. Even if Maman's family won't take us in, we'll find a home to stay in."

Shemmah got off her grandmother's lap as Otanes helped his mother up. "Yes, my son, you're correct. God

5

will provide a home for us, one way or another. Come, let's prepare for the journey ahead."

So in the twentieth year of Artaxerxes' reign, Sura, her son Otanes, his wife Shirin, their sons Babak, Narses, and daughter Shemmah started packing their belongings for the long journey ahead of them.

# A TIME FOR QUEEN VASHTI

## 2

The sound of a rooster crowing awoke Sura the next morning from a sound sleep. She had been dreaming of when she was young, when she was in the service of Queen Vashti and later Queen Esther. Her dream was so vivid, as if it had just happened. She and Shemmah shared a bed together, and as Sura stirred, she awoke Shemmah.

Shemmah rubbed her eyes and stretched her arms toward the ceiling. "Is everything okay, Maman-Bozorg?"

Sura loved looking into her granddaughter's bright, amber-colored eyes. They reminded her of the eyes of her deceased husband and her son's eyes. Shemmah's complexion was olive brown just like her father Otanes and her mother Shirin, but her hair was reddish-brown like Sura's had been in her youth.

Sura sat up, yawned and stretched. "Everything's fine, Shemmah. I was just dreaming."

Her granddaughter perked up. "What were you dreaming about?"

She pulled Shemmah close to her. "I was dreaming about the time I first came into the service of Queen Esther."

Shemmah started pulling on her grandmother's nightclothes. "Please, please, please tell me about it."

Sura patted Shemmah's hand. "Calm down, little one. I'll tell you about it; but then we need to get up and resume our packing."

The elderly woman's face beamed with love for her granddaughter as she started her story.

"It all started during the third year reign of King Xerxes, our present King Artaxerxes' father. I was one of Queen Vashti's servants at that time. She was the king's first wife. It has been forty years, but seems as if it were yesterday…"

"Sura, come quickly!" As Sura's friend, Chista, leaned out the window overlooking the king's square, she motioned with her hand for her to come over. "The criminal, Barsine, is being impaled on the gallows."

Sura was putting on her outer garment and grunted, clearly agitated. "Yes, I heard he had made plans to murder the king. Justice comes swiftly to those who wish to harm the king." Sura continued dressing, covering her hair with a head covering. Greatly annoyed, she chided, "I don't have time to watch, Chista, nor do I wish to see such savagery." As she quickly headed for the door of the servant's quarters, she almost tripped on her garment. "This has become a trying day!" she grumbled.

The queen had sent by courier a notice for Sura to serve at the feast she was having for women dignitaries from all of the king's provinces. Sura thought it was supposed to be Artunis, another servant girl, serving the queen, but there was a mix-up.

King Xerxes was also giving a feast in a different part of the palace for the high ranking men of his kingdom.

As Sura arrived on the veranda of the royal palace, the feast was well under way. The tables were low to the ground and beautifully set with ornate gold dishes, the finest purple linen tablecloths, and a large variety of pheasant and fruit. All the women were reclining on their couches, dining and enjoying their conversation.

Queen Vashti was known for her striking beauty. A multi-colored dress hugged her long, lean body. Her green eyes were bright and in lovely contrast to her golden-brown skin. The queen's blond waist-length hair had ribbons of different colors braided throughout which matched the colors in her dress.

The queen's eyes showed she was visibly angry. She asked, "Why are you late?"

Sura bowed and waited for the queen to motion for her to rise. "I just now received notice you requested my service. There was a mix-up in the servant's quarters. Please forgive me."

"Very well, then. Just don't let this happen again. Understand?" The queen gave her a stern look.

As the queen finished addressing Sura, one of the king's eunuchs (castrated man) entered the veranda.

"How many times have I told you not to disturb me when I'm entertaining my friends?" Queen Vashti huffed as she took another sip of tea.

"A thousand pardons, my queen," the eunuch proclaimed as he bowed before her, "but the king has requested you appear before his guests so they may gaze upon your beauty."

"You may tell the king I am more than just a pretty face for him to parade around those drunken nobles. He is asking me to unveil my face before all those men. He knows this is improper in our culture. I will not expose my face and my body to those men!"

The eunuch, Zethar, backed away bowing as he headed for the door and said, "As you wish, your majesty." Zethar rapidly returned to the king.

Sura positioned herself close to the queen and her guests and started playing her harp. As she was playing, Sura felt compelled to say something to the queen. Her youth and outspoken tongue often got her into trouble, yet she had difficulty bottling her feelings inside. "Your majesty, I understand it is not my place to say, but you know of the king's violent temper. Don't you think it would be in your best interest to go to his party as he requested?"

The queen snorted. "You are correct, Sura, it is not your place to say. Young one, you are interfering in affairs which are not your business. You know it is not proper for me as queen to expose my face and body to men unless they are family or a eunuch." The queen jumped up and pointed towards the door and said, "Off with you! Send me Artunis. She knows better than to speak up."

Sura entered the servants' quarters and spotted Artunis playing her harp. A year older than Sura, Artunis was fourteen, and in Persian culture, she was now of the age to marry. Her parents had arranged a marriage between her and Piruz. They were to marry in a few weeks.

Sura walked over to where Artunis was practicing. "Artunis, the queen has sent me to you. She wants you to play your harp for her and her guests on the veranda."

"Weren't you playing the harp for them? What did you do this time, Sura?" Artunis asked as she got up from her cushion. "Never mind. You can tell me about it when I get back."

All the girls in the servants' quarters were from ten to fifteen years old. Once the girls got married and had children, both they and their children had to work in the fields. They would no longer be in the service of the queen.

The girls gathered around Sura and watched her green eyes dart around as she told them what happened. Chista spoke up, "Sura, I know you mean well, but you don't want to make the queen angry again. Remember what happened last time you spoke up to the queen? She scolds you and you are put on the bottom of her list for playing the harp."

"Yes, you're right, Chista. I'll try to keep my mouth shut from now on, but it's so hard sometimes not to speak up," Sura said as she reached up to hug Chista's neck. Chista was much taller than her, with a very lean physique.

かひ

Zethar returned to the large room where the king and his guests were enjoying delicacies from surrounding nations. On the large, wooden carved table was a feast of roasted lamb, large bowls of dates, figs, and pomegranates as well as nan-e lavash (flat-bread), leeks, onions, and plenty of wine.

White and blue linen curtains were fastened with cords of fine linen and purple on silver rods and marble pillars. The couches were gold and silver on mosaic pavement. The king, clothed in royal purple apparel, was reclining on one of the couches surrounded by his closest companions: the seven princes of Persia and Media.

Zethar approached King Xerxes and bowed before him. He waited for the king to hold out the golden scepter. When the king held out his scepter, Zethar arose and the king asked him, "Why did Queen Vashti not return with you? Did I not command her to appear before my guests?"

"Yes, my lord, but the queen refused to come. She said she would not expose her face and body to these men."

The king jumped up from the couch. The part of his face not covered with his dark-brown beard was bright red with anger, and his dark-brown eyes changed to eyes of fire. In a drunken rage, he exclaimed, "How dare the queen dismiss my command!" As he waved his servant away, he turned to his closest companions and asked, "According to the law, what shall we do to Queen Vashti because she did not obey the command of King Xerxes?"

Memucan, one of the princes, stood up and addressed the king and his guests. Pacing back and forth, he stated, "Queen Vashti has not only wronged the king, but also all the princes, and all the men who are in the provinces of King Xerxes. The queen's behavior will become known to all women, so that they will not obey their husbands when they hear King Xerxes commanded Queen Vashti be brought in before him, but she did not come."

He continued, "If it pleases the king, may I suggest you write a royal decree and let it be recorded in the laws of the Persians and the Medes, so that it cannot be altered, that Vashti shall come no more before King Xerxes and let the king give her royal position to another who is better than she. You can have this decree proclaimed throughout the empire, so all wives will show honor to their husbands."

King Xerxes arose from the couch and kissed Memucan on each cheek as he held up his cup. "Is everyone in agreement?"

The princes all lifted their golden cups and took a drink in agreement to the new decree. King Xerxes then motioned for Zethar to approach. "Summon the scribe, Yousef, to come to me. Have him bring his parchment with him."

The king's 127 provinces received letters, each in their own script and language, affirming each man master in his own house.

A few days after the king banished Queen Vashti from his presence, he regretted his rash, drunken decision to make it a law for Vashti to never appear before him again. In Persia, once the king seals a legal document with his signet ring, the law could not be undone because as the representative of their god, Ormuzd, the king is looked upon as infallible.

# TIME TO SEARCH

3

Chista came running into the servant's quarters breathing heavily and almost stumbled and fell.

Sura jumped up off her floor cushion and asked, "What is it, Chista? Catch your breath and speak up!"

Chista tucked her brown hair back under her head covering. "It is rumored Queen Vashti has been executed. No one has seen her anywhere."

"Oh my," Sura remarked. "It sounds like once again the king's violent temper has resulted in someone's death."

As Chista put her hand on Sura's shoulder, she replied, "Whatever you do, you don't want to get on the king's bad side."

❧❦

Several days passed. Zethar placed the royal robe on the king and asked, "My lord, may I speak?"

King Xerxes nodded his head and gave approval. "Yes, Zethar, you may speak."

Zethar started pacing. "You need a queen, sire. It would be good to have beautiful young virgins sought for the king. Let us gather all the virgins here to the palace in Susa. You can put your eunuch, Hegai, as custodian of the women. The servant girls can make and apply the beauty preparations for these women. Then let the young woman who pleases the king be the new queen."

The king turned and faced Zethar with a smile. "This suggestion pleases me immensely. I will send a legion of officers to seek the most beautiful virgin out of each of my provinces, from India to Ethiopia, and have them brought here into the women's quarters under the care of Hegai."

Zethar bowed before the king and then left the room as the king continued to smile and look out the window at his beautifully manicured garden. "This is good. Good indeed."

∂∼∽

Mordecai could hear the sound of horses quickly approaching his residence. As he opened the door, he was startled to see an officer of the king's army standing there. The officer was of short stature, with broad muscular shoulders. Mordecai asked him, "May I be of assistance? What is it you are seeking?"

Farhad, the king's officer spoke. "King Xerxes has sent officers to seek the most beautiful virgin from all the king's provinces. He is seeking a queen to replace Vashti, the betrayer who dared to defy the king. I understand you have a beautiful virgin in your household."

The aging Mordecai spoke up, "I have raised my Uncle Abihail's daughter, Hadassah, as my own. She is at the market at this time."

Farhad entered Mordecai's residence and sat down in front of the fireplace, warming his hands by the fire, and took off his helmet. "Then I will wait here for her to return."

A short time later, Hadassah entered the house. The sun shining through the entrance danced off each strand of her long, golden-brown hair. With her tall, lean stature and a smile as bright as the midday sun, she was a beautiful sight to behold.

Coming home and seeing an officer with Mordecai greatly disturbed Hadassah. "Father, what is going on? Is everything okay?"

Mordecai wrinkled his brow with concern and then spoke, "My precious one, the officer is here to take you with him to the palace. The king is seeking a new queen and has ordered all beautiful virgins in his provinces be brought to the palace."

"Must I go? I can't stand the thought of leaving you all alone."

Farhad stood up, put his helmet back on, and said, "You must come with me now. Do not delay."

As Hadassah gave Mordecai a hug, he whispered into her ear, "Be careful to not let anyone know you are a Jew. It could prove to be detrimental to you."

Hadassah went outside with the officer and he placed her on a beautiful, white horse that had a red and gold-colored tapestry on its back. With tears streaming down her lightly-tanned face, she waved farewell to Mordecai and the life she once knew.

As they approached the palace, Hadassah noticed a guard on each side of the twenty-foot doors. Each man wore armor and held a long spear in their hand protecting the entrance to the palace. When they opened the doors, Hadassah observed opulence she had never seen before. The walls were overlaid with gold-relief carvings of lions, bulls, and open flowers. The floors were white marble with gold veins running through each large tile.

"We are here; let me help you dismount." Farhad placed a step near the horse for Hadassah to dismount on.

Hegai, the eunuch, came out of the women's residence of the palace to greet the new arrival. He was a very large, bald man, with dark skin, and though his presence was felt by all, there was a gentleness about him.

"Here is another virgin for you to oversee in the women's quarters, Hegai," Farhad announced as Hadassah approached the eunuch.

"What is your name young miss?" Hegai asked.

"My father calls me Hadassah, but you Persians call me Esther."

"Ah yes, Esther—a star. We shall soon see if you do indeed live up to the meaning of your name. Come with me."

As Farhad departed, Esther followed Hegai into the women's quarters. She entered the quarters and saw more than a hundred virgins, each being waited on by servant girls. The girls were applying oils and perfumes on the virgins. They were brushing and braiding their hair and helping them with their beautiful silk dresses.

Seven young servant girls walked up to Esther. Sura was in charge of the girls and spoke up. "We are here at your service, madam."

"Madam? I am not much older than you. You may call me Esther."

"As you wish, Esther. My name is Sura, and this is Chista, Roxana, Pari, Banu, Atusa, and Zand." Each of the girls bowed before Esther, and as they backed away they remained standing. "As I said before, we are here at your service."

"Thank you, Sura and girls." Esther looked around the very large room and the ornate décor and watched the servants attending to the other beautiful virgins. "All this attention and the lavish surroundings are foreign to me. I believe you girls will help me adjust to this new life."

The girls continued to stand before Esther until Hegai spoke up. "They are waiting for you to dismiss them."

"Oh." She smiled at the girls and said, "You may go now."

Hegai quickly took a special liking to Esther. She was not only beautiful on the outside, but her bright blue eyes shined with the beauty she had within.

Hegai walked towards a double-door that opened into a room with several beds with white netting around them and said, "Follow me to your bed chamber you'll be sharing with some girls from the Northern Province."

As Hegai and Esther entered the room, she observed each girl with her distinct look. Esther walked up to one of the girls and noticed her long, black hair glistened from the beauty treatments she had received, and her dark-brown eyes sparkled with anticipation.

Esther smiled and said, "May you have peace."

"Peace to you. My name is Mandana, and I am from the Gilan province."

"Yes, I've heard about the Gilan province. It is by the Caspian Sea and has beautiful forests and mountains."

Mandana cocked her head to one side and slightly opened her mouth, surprised Esther was familiar with her obscure province. "You are correct. Where did you hear of Gilan?"

Esther answered her confidently, "I heard about it when I received my schooling here in Susa."

Mandana lowered her head. "Girls in my province are not allowed to obtain schooling. You are very fortunate."

Esther smiled a big smile. "Yes, my God has shined his face on me my whole life."

"Well, Esther, I am sure we will become good friends as we share this room together. Maybe you can teach me some of the things you learned."

Esther gave Mandana a hug. "I would love to teach you, Mandana. I believe all girls should be educated, not just the boys."

ॐॐ

Each day Hegai supplied Esther with parchments so she could write about her adventure in the palace. She also taught Mandana letters of the alphabet. Mandana was a quick learner, and in a few months she was able to read.

"Thank you, Esther, for teaching me to read and write." Mandana wiped a tear from her eye and asked, "Do you think it would be possible to send a letter to my parents in Gilan?"

Esther motioned for Sura to approach. "Sura, please go and ask the courier, Babar, when he will be delivering letters to the Gilan Province."

"Yes, Esther."

On her way to get Babar, Sura ran into Farhad in the king's garden.

"Peace to you, Sura."

Sura shyly looked down and answered, "Peace to you, Farhad."

Farhad continued, "You look especially lovely today. Your beauty surpasses the flowers in the king's garden."

Sura's face turned many shades of red, and as she turned away, she answered, "Thank you."

"Wait, don't go! Our parents have arranged our wedding to take place next year, and then you will be my wife. I know you don't know me very well, but you will see I will treat you with kindness."

She looked into his amber-colored eyes. They did look kind, and he had a handsome smile. "I have heard good things about you and how you help the poor. I trust my parents' judgment."

An officer walked up to Farhad and saluted. "The king has ordered us to duty outside the city gate. Quickly, we must go!"

Farhad left her side and told her, "Farewell my love. Soon we unite in marriage."

Sura's heart quickened as he left. She was looking forward to marriage and children, but not to a life outside the palace walls, to a life of hard labor working in the fields.

Sura continued to the courier's station and saw Babar lounging at a long table enjoying his morning cup of tea.

He remained lounging and asked, "Yes, young miss; may I be of assistance?"

"I am in the service of Esther, one of the king's virgins. She sent me to find out when you would be delivering letters to the Gilan Province."

"In just a couple of days I will be taking letters from the king to the Gilan Province."

"Thank you. Would you be as kind as to deliver a letter from Esther's friend to her parents in the Gilan Province?"

Babar sat up and asserted, "It would be my pleasure."

Esther helped Mandana write the letter to her parents. The kindness Esther showed to Mandana and all the virgins in the women's quarters surpassed everyone. Everyone in the women's quarters was touched by how kind Esther was.

∂∞6

It took a whole year to prepare the virgins for their appearance before the king. Hegai made sure Esther had plenty of beauty preparations available for her.

Esther and Sura became very fond of each other. When Sura was not applying beauty treatments on Esther, she would play the harp for her.

Sura was playing the harp for Esther early one morning when she started talking to the young virgin. "Esther, for a year now a man who says he raised you, paces in front of the court of the women's quarters asking how you are and what is happening to you. Every day, I give him a report on your welfare."

"He is Mordecai, and I call him my father. I want him to know I'm all right. Thank you for keeping him informed about my welfare."

Esther turned and noticed Mandana was very nicely adorned and ready to appear before the king. The oils applied to her made her skin glow like the moon in a darkened sky.

Esther watched Mandana and wondered out loud, "There have been over a hundred virgins who have stood before the king, and still no queen. I wonder what he is looking for in a woman."

Sura spoke up, "I don't know what he is looking for, but I do know you are more special than all the other women. You are different. You don't treat me as a servant, but as your friend."

"Sura, you live up to the meaning of your name. You have a beautiful face, like a beautiful flower, soft and white. Your eyes are as green as emeralds. One day you will have a handsome husband and beautiful children who will look just like you."

Sura met Esther's eyes and then sadly looked away.

"What is it, Sura?"

As she twisted her reddish-brown hair around her finger she replied, "My father and mother have arranged for me to marry soon. I am to marry Farhad."

"Ah yes, Farhad. Isn't he the king's officer who brought me here to the palace?"

"Yes, he is the one."

"Well, Sura, this is good news. He should bring you much happiness. After all, his name means happiness."

Sura started pacing. "That is not why I'm sad. After I marry and have children, I will no longer be in your service. I will have to work in the fields with the other servants."

Esther tenderly cupped her hands around Sura's face and looked into her eyes. "Oh, Sura, I will pray to my God that such a thing will not occur."

Sura watched as Esther went up to Mandana and said, "You look beautiful. I am so glad I have had you in my life this past year. May you be successful before the king."

Mandana wiped a tear from her eye. "Oh, Esther, you continually look out for the other person, with no regard for yourself." She gave Esther a hug then continued, "May you be blessed."

❧

The next morning Hegai informed Esther that Mandana was not chosen as queen, and she was now in the custody of the king's eunuch, Shaashgaz who was in charge of the king's concubines.

Esther remembered the good talks she and Mandana had over the past year. She sat down on the edge of her bed and sighed, "Oh, Hegai, I feel terrible for Mandana. She will live the rest of her life as just a concubine."

"In the service of the king, there are worse things than being his concubine. At least she will have the luxury of the palace, much different from how she lived in the Gilan Province."

Hegai took her by the hand and lifted her up, "Enough of this! Tonight is your night to appear before the king." Hegai called Sura with a loud voice. "Sura, come quickly! You and the other servants need to start preparing Esther for her appearance before the king tonight."

The girls started preparing Esther early that morning. After a year of preparation, her skin glowed like a sun-kissed meadow, her hair glistened like light dancing on a clear, mountain lake, and her teeth were as white as snow.

Roxana filled a large copper vessel with water she had heated in the fireplace. Pari took a mixture of frankincense and myrrh and poured it into the bath. Esther gingerly stepped into the tub and sat down. Atusa gently massaged the oil over Esther's body. When Atusa finished, Esther stood up and Banu brought a linen cloth and dried her off.

Finally, it was time to dress Esther for the occasion. The dress chosen was woven by Esther herself. It was silk, long and flowing, soft pink in color with jasmine flowers embroidered throughout. Chista helped Esther put on her dress, and Sura worked on her hair. Her golden-brown hair was one long braid with tiny white flowers tucked into it.

Sura placed the last flower into Esther's hair. Tears formed and started rolling down her cheek. "Esther, the day you've been preparing for a year now has arrived. You are so beautiful."

Esther gave Sura a hug, and both started weeping as Hegai walked through the large, carved cedar doors leading into the women's quarters.

"What a beautiful flower you have become, Esther. Dry your tears and come with me. The king will be quite pleased with you. It's time to appear before the king. You too, Sura; he has requested you serve them."

They entered through the twelve-foot golden doors leading to the king's chamber. One of the king's eunuchs, Armand, struck a bronze gong announcing Esther's arrival.

Hegai took Esther to the king, who was reclining on his couch overlooking the balcony. She approached the king, and he stood up. Esther noticed he was tall, and had a commanding presence about him. After he stood up he started walking all around her, looking her over – every inch.

The king motioned for Hegai and Armand to leave. Only Esther, the king, and Sura remained in the room.

King Xerxes, clothed in his regal apparel, wore a purple silk inner garment and a vest woven with threads of gold and silver. On his head was a crown with precious rubies, sapphires, and pearls. He appeared to Esther as dark and mysterious, with his dark-brown beard and eyes. He looked into Esther's beautiful, blue eyes and asked her, "What is your name, my dear one?"

Esther started to answer. She lowered her head and her eyes. The king gently lifted her head back up with his hand under her chin.

"It's okay, my dear; don't be afraid. I won't hurt you. Tell me, what is your name?"

"My name is Esther, your majesty."

"Yes, I can see why you have this name. It suits you well. Come recline with me on the couch." He snapped his fingers, and Sura ran up to him.

"Play your harp for Esther and me."

"Yes, your majesty."

Esther joined the king on the couch as Sura played her harp.

The king looked intently into Esther's eyes. "Tell me about your family and where you grew up."

Esther looked into the king's eyes. "My parents died when I was quite young. My older cousin raised me as his own daughter, right here in Susa."

The king picked up Esther's hand and cupped it in his. He asked her, "Tell me, did you receive an education?"

Esther smiled and answered, "Yes, your majesty. I have learned to read and write, and I'm proficient at weaving."

The king reached out and touched her dress. "Did you weave this?"

Esther smiled once more and answered, "I did weave this, my king. I hope you like it."

King Xerxes could not help but smile also. "I do indeed like it. I have heard very good reports of your behavior with all the virgins in the women's quarters. I understand you are kind to all."

"My king, I believe you should treat all people with kindness and compassion. I have found when you are kind to others, they generally are kind to you."

The king listened to Esther talk about her family, her education, and growing up in Susa. He listened to her while staring at her beautiful face and ogling her shapely body. She was not only beautiful, but her intelligence, her candidness, and her sweet disposition made the king instantly fall in love with Esther. After talking for a couple of hours to Esther, he motioned for Sura.

"Yes, my king."

The king arose from the couch and pointed to a table close to his bed. "Bring me the queen's crown."

Sura returned with a golden crown in her hand and gave it to the king.

King Xerxes placed the crown on Esther's head and said, "I choose you as my queen."

Esther bowed and replied, "May I only bring honor to you and your kingdom as your queen, my lord."

The king motioned for Sura once more. "Girl, have the servants prepare a great feast for this special occasion. The feast shall be called the Feast of Esther. Have them work through the night and tomorrow. Make sure all the preparations are completed by dusk tomorrow."

# TIME TO SEARCH IS OVER

## 4

Morning came, and there was much excitement around the palace as word spread about the new queen. All of the servants were busy preparing for the wedding feast, each with his or her own task. Sura and the other attendants adorned Esther in her wedding attire. Her dress was white silk with tiny lilac flowers embroidered on it. She wore a sheer lilac-colored head covering loosely wrapped around her neck. A gold crown full of precious gems of various colors was on her head.

The wedding took place at dusk in the throne room, with both dignitaries and servants attending. More than five hundred people were in attendance, and the wedding was celebrated according to Persian tradition.

Esther entered the room and sat on her throne next to the king's throne. He took her hands and kissed them. The two ate from the same loaf of bread sliced in two parts by a sword wielded by one of the servants, and they drank some wine. After many hours of celebration, the king proclaimed it a holiday, which would last for one week, and gave gifts according to his generosity to both great and small.

After the ceremony the king took his new queen into his bed chamber and closed the door. He took Esther into his big, strong arms and held her there for a moment.

"You are most beautiful, my love. At the feast, I could not take my eyes off of you. I promise to treat you tender, forever," the king proclaimed as he looked into her eyes.

Queen Esther looked with love at this man who was treating her so kind. "And I, my dear husband, will in all ways show you the honor you deserve."

ॐ᠊ঔ

The servant girls were still giddy from the wedding feast. They all gathered together in the women's quarters showing each other their gifts from the king.

Zand paraded around in her new dress, Banu had a new golden ring in her nose, Pari danced around in her new shoes, and Chista twirled around with her new shawl wrapped over her long, brown hair.

Chista spoke up, "What did you receive, Sura? It must have been special, for the queen took a liking to you."

"Yes, I am fortunate. The queen is requesting that the king not banish me to the fields after Farhad and I marry and have children. If he grants her request, I will remain in her service."

"Oh, Sura, how fortunate you are. I am so happy for you, but all of us girls are now of marrying age, and we will soon be leaving the palace." Christa wiped tears from her big, brown eyes and said, "I will never forget you."

The girls formed a circle around Sura and took turns hugging her.

Sura started weeping. "It's not fair I receive special treatment just because the queen took a liking to me. If it is possible, while in the queen's service, I will try to persuade the queen to discuss with the king about changing this law. May we all be able to remain in the palace."

"What have I told you about speaking up to the royalty, Sura?" Chista took Sura's hand and held it up. "Swear to me you will stop this nonsense. Just accept your good fortune and don't risk your neck for us."

Sura jerked her hand away. She told her, "I will not swear to anything. You don't understand. Queen Esther is different from any royalty I've ever met. She treats even her servants as her equal."

"People change, Sura. That is what happens when people get a taste of position and power. Queen Esther will change too," Chista affirmed.

"Chista, you are my best friend, but you are wrong about Queen Esther. You will see."

❦

Not many days after the feast, Mordecai sat within the king's gate and overheard plans by two of the king's eunuchs, Bigthan and Teresh, to murder King Xerxes. They were doorkeepers who protected the entrance into the throne room. The plan was to wait until no one else was in the throne room and the king had a few cups of wine. Then they would go behind him and slit his throat.

When the plot became known to Mordecai, he told Queen Esther, and Esther informed the king in Mordecai's name.

The matter was investigated and confirmed. Both men were impaled on a gallows. The scribe, while with the king, wrote about the plot and its outcome in the book of the chronicles of the king.

ॐॐ

Queen Esther requested a new law which would allow the servant girls in service at the palace to stay after marriage and bearing children. The king, quite taken with Esther's beauty and intelligence, granted her request.

When Sura heard the news she came almost running into the women's quarters. "Chista, did you hear? Did you girls hear the news?"

Only Chista, Zand, and Banu were there at the time. Chista asked, "What news?"

Sura was dancing around; she couldn't contain her happiness. "We can stay. All of us!"

Zand asked, "What are you talking about?"

Sura took a deep breath. "Just like I told you girls, Queen Esther is a friend of servant girls. She requested a law which would allow us to stay in the palace after marriage and children, and the king granted her request."

Shemmah interrupted her grandma Sura, "Maman-Bozorg, is this when you married Baba-Bozorg?"

"You are correct, my dear child. I married your grandfather, Farhad, and a year later your father was born, and I was still able to serve Queen Esther due to the new law. My friend Chista also got married and she had several children. We both remained in the service of the queen. Now, no more interruptions; let me continue with the story..."

On the day Sura's son, Otanes, was born, Chista was assisting Sura with the birth of the child. Sura's husband Farhad was there as was her mother-in-law, Amitis. Sura's Persian parents had both died shortly after her marriage to Farhad from complications from the flu.

"Push, Sura—harder! That's it; I can see his head," Chista declared as she pulled gently on the baby's head.

"*His* head?" Farhad asked.

*WAAAH—WAAAH—WAAAH.* "Yes, it's a boy!" Chista laid the baby on Sura's chest. Sura was weeping for joy as she held her baby for the first time.

Farhad went to Sura's side, kissed her forehead, and then the baby's. "What shall we name him?"

Sura kissed her baby. "I've been thinking; how about Otanes?"

Farhad was filled with joy. "Oh Sura, that's wonderful. My father would have been so proud to have our child named after him. Yes, Otanes it is."

Amitis started crying. "I am so happy. Once again I will hear the name Otanes. This is a special name indeed."

The queen provided her servants family quarters to reside with their families within the palace. When she heard about Sura's delivery of a healthy, baby boy she was thrilled. She sent her servants Banu and Zand to Sura bearing gifts for the child.

Banu walked through the door of Sura's home with excitement. "The queen is delighted to hear of the birth of your son and has sent this cradle…"

Zand spoke up, "And all these clothes for the baby."

Sura could hardly contain all the happiness she had in her heart. "Please tell the queen, words cannot express how grateful I am for her generosity."

❧

The years passed and Sura remained in the service of the queen. When Sura was serving the queen and Farhad was away fighting battles for the king, Sura's mother-in-law cared for Otanes.

After just a few years of marriage, Farhad, at the king's command, went to an uprising in a distant country. He died serving there. Sura's mother-in-law was so distraught when she received the news that her son had died in battle, she had a heart attack and died. Sura was now a widow with a young son to raise on her own. Those were difficult years for her, but the queen continued to show kindness to Sura and to her son.

# TIME OF HATE

5

A round the time Farhad died in battle, King Xerxes promoted a man by the name of Haman and advanced him above all the princes who were with him.

All the king's servants who were within the king's gate bowed and paid homage to Haman, except for Esther's father, Mordecai. He would not bow or pay homage.

Some of the king's servants asked Mordecai, "Why do you not follow the king's command and pay homage to Haman?"

Mordecai answered, "I am a Jew, and I do not bow or pay homage to any man, only to my God, Jehovah."

When Haman saw Mordecai continued not to bow or pay homage to him, Haman filled with rage. He decided the best way to get rid of Mordecai was to destroy all the Jews who were throughout the entire kingdom of Xerxes— the people of Mordecai.

In the first month of the year, Haman and his servants cast Pur (or lots) to decide which month the Jews would be destroyed. The lots landed on the twelfth month, which is the month of Adar on the Jewish calendar.

Then Haman said to King Xerxes, "There is a certain people scattered and dispersed throughout all the provinces of your kingdom." Haman looked out the window, then turned and faced the king once more. "Their laws are different from all other people's laws, and they disregard the king's laws. Therefore, if it pleases the king, let a decree be written that they be destroyed."

The king was furious. "Who are these people who defy the king's laws?"

Haman smirked. "They are Jews. I'll pay for their annihilation myself and deposit ten thousand talents of silver into the king's treasury to finance the operation."

"Yes, Haman, this pleases me. You have my blessing." The king took his signet ring from his hand and gave it to Haman. "It's your money—do whatever you want with those people."

The king then ordered the scribes to write a decree according to all that Haman commanded. The decree was then sealed with the king's signet ring. It was sent by couriers to every province in the king's kingdom and to every people in their own language. The decree called for annihilation of all Jews, both young and old, men, women, and children. The massacre would take place in one day, on the thirteenth day of the month of Adar. The Jews had one year to make themselves ready for their destruction. There was much crying and commotion throughout all the provinces. Many lay in sackcloth and ashes as was the Jewish custom in times of deep distress.

When Mordecai learned all that had happened, he tore his clothes, put on sackcloth and ashes, and went out into the midst of the city. He went as far as the square in front of the king's gate crying out with a loud voice.

Sura went to Queen Esther and told her about Mordecai. "Your father is crying, and he is wearing sackcloth and ashes in the king's square. Is there anything I can do to help?"

The queen was deeply distressed and said, "I don't know why he is acting like that. I'll send you with new clothing for Mordecai and be sure to take his sackcloth clothing from him."

Mordecai was sitting in the king's square as Sura walked up to him. His gray hair and beard were covered with the sackcloth. "Sir, Queen Esther has sent a change of clothing for you. Please accept this gift from the queen."

"You don't understand. I'm in mourning. Take away the clothes! I don't want them. Go and leave me alone."

When Sura told Queen Esther that Mordecai would not take the clothing and was in mourning, she sent Armand, one of the king's eunuchs, to Mordecai to find out what his behavior was all about.

Mordecai arose from his seat in the king's square and began to explain all the events which had taken place. He told Armand about the sum of money Haman promised to pay into the king's treasuries to destroy the Jews.

He handed him a copy of the written decree calling for the Jews destruction and urged him, "Armand, it's important for you to give this to the queen and tell her everything I have told you. She must go before the king and plead before him for her people."

So Armand returned and told Esther all Mordecai had told him. After several years of marriage, the king spent many days away from Susa fighting his enemies in other countries. When he was home he was busy with his kingly duties. He seldom requested for the queen to appear before him.

"Armand, you must tell Mordecai I have not been called to go in to the king for thirty days now. I don't know if I still find favor with him or not. It is well-known throughout all the provinces, any man or woman who goes into the inner court to the king, who has not been called, he has but one law—death, unless the king holds out his golden scepter. Surly there is another way. Go, tell Mordecai this."

Mordecai saw Armand approaching and motioned for him to sit with him under an elm tree. "Tell me, how did the queen respond?"

Once again Armand told Mordecai what Esther had said.

Mordecai stood up and started pacing. "You will tell the queen, there is no other way. If she thinks she will escape destruction being in the king's palace any more than the others, she is mistaken. She must see that perhaps this is the reason she has been chosen as Queen…for such a time like this."

Queen Esther was looking out the window, waiting for the return of Armand. He entered her quarters and she walked over to him. He told her what Mordecai had said. She in response told him, "Go, and gather all the Jews who are present in Susa and tell them to fast for me. Neither eat nor drink for three days, night or day. My maidens and I shall fast likewise. Afterwards, I will go to the king, which is against the law; and if I perish, I perish!"

# TIME TO BANQUET

6

All the Jews in Susa did according to Queen Esther's request and fasted, night and day, for three days. They called upon their God, Jehovah, to save them from annihilation.

On the third day, all of the girls in the service of Queen Esther prepared a bountiful banquet at her command. It consisted of lamb baked with herbs, much bread, a large variety of fruit from the king's garden, and much wine.

Queen Esther put on her royal robe and stood in the inner court of the king's palace, across from the king's house. The king was sitting on his throne in the royal house, which faced the entrance of the house. When the king saw Queen Esther standing in the court, she found favor in his sight. The king held out his golden scepter to Esther. She went near, bowed, and touched the top of the scepter.

She stood before him, and he asked, "What do you wish, Queen Esther? What is your request? It shall be given to you—up to half my kingdom!"

Esther bravely answered the king, "Thank you my lord, but if it pleases the king, my request is for the presence of yourself and Haman to come today to a banquet I have prepared for you both. I would be honored to have you and Haman attend."

The king got up from the royal throne and approached Queen Esther. "Once again I find you intriguing. You could have had up to half of my kingdom, yet all you ask is for Haman and me to attend your banquet."

King Xerxes motioned for his servant Armand. "Bring Haman quickly so he may attend this banquet the queen has prepared."

So both the king and Haman went to the banquet Esther had prepared for them.

At the banquet, Armand poured wine into their cups, and Sura played her harp for them. The king, being in a generous mood, asked Esther once again, "What would you like? I'll grant you anything you want—up to half of my kingdom. Just tell me, and it shall be done!"

Queen Esther leaned back on the couch, and with her face close to the king's, she answered, "My only request is this. If I have found favor in the sight of the king, I would like to prepare another banquet tomorrow for you, my lord, and for Haman. I would be honored, once again, to have your presence."

The king looked into the queen's beautiful blue eyes. She was especially beautiful today, wearing a cream-colored silk dress, with hyacinths embroidered on the dress. He kissed her on her forehead and said, "No, it is I who would be honored to once again be in the presence of such beauty. We will both attend."

෨ൟ

After Haman left the banquet, he started walking through the king's gardens toward the king's gate. He had drunk too much wine and was stumbling around.

He stopped one of the princes, Meres, to tell him of his good fortune. "Not only did the queen resquest my presence at today's bansquet," He was slurring his words, "But swee is having another one tomorrow whisch I am to attend."

Meres walked beside Haman, and as they neared the king's gate, Meres replied, "Seems odd. I've never heard of the queen ever having two banquets together, one right after another."

Haman put his hand on Meres shoulder, which Meres quickly took off. "I tell you, Meres," Haman continued in his drunken stupor, "The squeen likes me."

All of a sudden, Haman's countenance changed from joyful to anger. As he passed through the king's gate, everyone bowed to pay homage to him, everyone except for Mordecai.

Meres spoke up. "Why are you so angry? You got your desire. In only eleven more months, Mordecai and all the Jews will be annihilated. Isn't that what you wanted?"

Haman tried to restrain himself, but whispered to Meres, "Eleven months is not soon enough."

Haman entered his home and called for his wife. "Zeresh, tell Sheta to go knock on our friends' doors and gather all our relatives together. Have Sheta tell them I have good news to share with them."

By the time his friends and relatives arrived, Haman's wife had set a table with bread, figs, and wine.

Haman, in his drunkenness, began to brag, "Look how the gods have blessed me, yes, above all. I have ten sons, much gold, and the king has promoted me above all the officials and servants of the king."

He got up, stumbled, and almost landed in his wife's lap. "Besides, Queen Esther invited no one but me to come in and banquet with her and the king. Tomorrow, I'm again invited by her, along with the king."

Haman sat back down. "None of this avails me as long as I continue to see Mordecai the Jew sitting in the king's gate. How dare him not bow and pay homage to me!"

Haman's wife and all his friends discussed it among themselves and came up with a plan.

Zeresh started, "Let a gallows be made seventy-five feet high…"

Datar, a friend of Haman continued, "Yes, and in the morning suggest to the king that Mordecai be hanged on it. Then you can enjoy your banquet knowing this scum is no more."

Haman jumped up excitedly. "Sheta, you and the other servants go gather the wood you need and have this erected by dawn. It will be so tall, the entire city will see Mordecai hanging from it."

৵৽

The night progressed, and the king was having difficulty sleeping, so he called for his servant. "Armand, bring me the book of the records of the chronicles and have Zethar read them to me."

Armand returned with the book and Zethar. After a couple of hours of reading, Zethar came to the part where

Mordecai told about Bigthana and Teresh, the king's eunuchs, and their plot to kill the king.

The king asked Zethar, "Was any honor bestowed on Mordecai for this?"

Zethar searched the book and answered, "None my king."

By this time, dawn had broken, and the king could see by the early light there was someone in his outer court. The king asked, "Who is in the court?"

Zethar answered the king, "Haman is standing in the court."

The king held out his scepter and said, "Let him come in."

Haman had come to the outer court of the king's palace to suggest the king hang Mordecai on the enormous gallows he had erected.

Haman entered the throne room, and the king asked him, "What shall be done for the man whom the king delights to honor?"

All Haman could think was, *whom would the king delight to honor more than me? No one.*

"For the man whom the king delights to honor," Haman stuck out his chest and cleared his throat, "Ahem, let one of the king's royal robes be brought, and one of the king's horses he had ridden, with a royal crown on its head. Let one of your most noble princes array this man and then parade him on horseback through the city proclaiming: 'Thus shall it be done to the man whom the king delights to honor!'"

"Very well then, go and do it." The king arose and pointed towards the door. "Don't waste another minute. Take the robe and horse and do what you have proposed to

Mordecai the Jew who sits at the King's Gate. Don't leave anything out of your plan."

Haman's brown eyes turned red with anger. He turned away from the king briefly and composed himself.

So Haman took the robe and horse, placed the robe on Mordecai, and led him through the city square proclaiming before him, "Thus shall it be done to the man whom the king delights to honor!"

When Haman returned from parading Mordecai on horseback through the city square, Mordecai went back to the king's gate. Haman covered his dark hair in mourning and quickly went home. When Haman finished telling his wife Zeresh and all his friends everything that had happened, some of his knowledgeable friends told him, "With Mordecai being a Jew, your bad luck has only begun. You don't stand a chance; you're as good as dead."

They were still talking when one of the king's eunuchs arrived and hurried Haman to the second banquet Esther had prepared.

# FOR THE SECOND TIME

7

So the king and Haman went to dine with Queen Esther. At the banquet Sura was there once again playing her instrument and singing. They were drinking wine when the king again asked, "What would you like, Queen Esther—up to half my kingdom? Ask and it is yours."

The queen leaned back and looked into the king's eyes. "If I have found favor in your eyes, my lord, and if it pleases the king, give me and my people's lives back. We've been sold, my people and I, sold to be annihilated. If sold into slavery, I wouldn't even have brought it up, for our troubles wouldn't have been worth bothering the king over."

King Xerxes jumped up from the couch and asked, "Who is the one who did this, and where is he? This is monstrous!"

"The man is this evil man Haman!" Queen Esther sat up and pointed to Haman, who was terror-stricken before the king and queen.

The king was raging and yelling obscenities. He left his wine and went into the palace garden to think. Haman remained in front of Queen Esther pleading for his life, for he could see he was slated to die.

The king returned from the garden into the banquet hall. Haman had fallen across the couch where Esther was. The king was furious. "What! Are you trying to molest the queen with me just around the corner?"

All the color left Haman's face, and his body went limp.

Armand pointed out the window towards Haman's house. "Look, my lord! There's the seventy-five feet high gallows that Haman had built for Mordecai, who saved the king's life."

The king spoke up, "Hang him on it!"

ᏽᏽ

The next day, they hanged Haman on the very gallows that he had built for Mordecai. Then the king's anger subsided.

On that very day, King Xerxes gave Queen Esther the estate of Haman, the enemy of the Jews. Mordecai appeared before the king because Esther explained how he had raised her like a father. The king took off his signet ring, which he had taken back from Haman, and gave it to Mordecai. Esther appointed Mordecai over Haman's estate.

Then Esther fell down at the king's feet, begging with tears to counteract the evil plan Haman had plotted against the Jews. The king extended his golden scepter to Esther. She stood up and implored the king, "If it pleases you, my king, and you regard me with favor and think this is right, and if you have any affection for me at all, let an order be written that cancels the letters devised by Haman, which he wrote to annihilate the Jews who are in the king's provinces. For how can I stand to see this catastrophe wipe out my people? Or how can I bear to stand by and watch the massacre of my own relatives?"

King Xerxes stood up and cupped Queen Esther's face in his hands. Mordecai looked on as the king said, "Indeed, I have given you, my love, the house of Haman, and my servants have hanged Haman on the gallows because of his plot against the Jews. You and Mordecai write a decree for the Jews, as is good in your eyes, in the king's name. Mordecai, you seal it with the signet ring which I gave you, for a decree written in the king's name and sealed with the king's signet ring cannot be revoked."

&#8667;&#8669;

The king's scribes wrote down word for word as Mordecai dictated. The decree was addressed to the satraps, governors, and officials of the one hundred twenty-seven provinces King Xerxes ruled over. Written in each province's own script and language, the word quickly spread. The document allowed the Jews in every province to gather together and defend themselves to the death from any forces trying to assault them on the thirteenth day of Adar.

The order, written in King Xerxes' name and sealed with his signet ring, went to all the provinces by couriers riding on royal horses bred from swift steeds. This order was also posted in the palace complex in Susa. The people of Susa celebrated with joy. In every city of every province when the king's order came, the Jews were cheering and feasting.

❧❦

"Armand, what a joyous occasion this is!" King Xerxes exclaimed as he watched the celebration through the window. "Tell the queen's servant girl, Sura, to bring Mordecai here."

"My lord," Esther proclaimed as she joined the king at the window, "I am so overjoyed. You have provided a means of escape for my people from those who wish to harm them. How can I ever repay you?"

He pulled her in close to him, kissed her and said, "Your beauty, inside and out, reflects the God you serve. It is payment enough; more precious than gold, or silver."

The king and queen were still watching from the window when Mordecai and Sura walked in.

Sura announced Mordecai's arrival to the king and queen, "Your majesties, Mordecai has arrived."

"Sura, pour us all some wine," the king commanded as he walked over to Mordecai.

"I am honoring you by making you second in command," the king snapped his fingers. "Sura, when you have finished pouring the wine, go retrieve from the royal wardrobe, the royal attire I have had laid out for Mordecai."

"Yes, my lord."

When Sura returned with the royal garments, the king gave them to Mordecai, who left the king's presence wearing a royal robe of blue and white, a huge gold crown, and a purple cape of fine linen.

❧◆❧

Sura was in the throne room with the king and queen serving them on the thirteenth day of Adar, the day the king's order came into effect. That evening the queen paced back and forth as the king spoke to her, "My precious one, come sit beside me. Word will come soon, and I'm sure it will be good news for you and your people."

"Yes, my lord, I'm sure you are correct. I know our God, Jehovah, will protect his people."

"Sura," the king snapped his fingers, "pour us both some wine."

"Yes, your majesty."

Sura poured the wine when the king again spoke with the queen, "This is the day the enemies of the Jews planned to annihilate them, but…"

The king was still talking when Armand entered the room. The king extended his scepter to Armand.

"Sire, news comes from here in Susa. The Jews overpowered their enemies. Not one man was able to stand up against them. All the government officials, satraps, governors—all helped the Jews. In the palace complex alone, the Jews have killed five hundred men, plus Haman's ten sons."

The king cupped his hands around the queen's hands. "This is good news indeed, my queen. Think of the massacre which must have taken place in the rest of the provinces! What else can I do for you? Name it and it is yours."

Queen Esther responded, "If it pleases the king, extend the order another day here in Susa, and have the bodies of Haman's sons hanged in public display on the gallows as an example of what will happen should anyone come against my people."

"Armand," the king stood up, "you heard the queen. Send me the scribes to write an extension of the order, and for the bodies of Haman's sons to be hanged as the queen suggested."

"Yes, sire."

രുൽ

The following day, the fourteenth of Adar, the Jews killed another three hundred men in Susa. After several days passed, the couriers returned from the rest of the king's provinces with the news that the Jews killed 75,000 people who hated them. Mordecai then called for a scribe.

Yousef, one of the king's scribes appeared before Mordecai, "Yes, my lord, you called for me?"

"Write down the outcome of the order of the king, both here in Susa and in all the king's provinces. Also, I am calling for an annual celebration on the fourteenth and fifteenth day of Adar as the occasion when we Jews got relief from our enemies. This will be a time for parties, the sending and receiving of presents, and of giving gifts to the poor. The celebration will be called 'Purim' from the word *pur* or 'lot', for Haman had cast pur to choose the day of destruction of the Jews, only to have it return on his own head."

❧❧

"Maman-Bozorg, so is this where we get the celebration of Purim from."

"Yes, my sweet, little Shemmah. I was there with Queen Esther as she used her full queenly authority to endorse and ratify what Mordecai wrote. Letters went out to all the Jews throughout all the provinces of King Xerxes' kingdom to fix these days of Purim their assigned place on the calendar. All of these events are written in The Chronicles of the Kings of Media and Persia."

"Is this when we became Jews too?"

"Your baba and I were born Jews; but many Persians did become Jews at this time, including your maman, Shirin. The Persians saw the hand of our God, Jehovah, the hand of providence. He has worked this same hand of providence in our own lives too. Many times in these past forty years we came close to destruction, but God was with us. King David wrote in the Psalms, 'The Lord is near to all who call upon Him in truth; He will fulfill the desires of those who fear Him; He also will hear their cry and save them. The Lord preserves all who love Him, but all the wicked He will destroy.'"

"What happened to King Xerxes and Queen Esther, Maman-Bozorg?"

"King Xerxes died several years after Haman tried to annihilate the Jews. His love for no other was as strong as his love for Queen Esther. The queen now serves as an advisor to her son King Artaxerxes."

# LONG-TIME FRIENDS

## 8

Sura and her granddaughter got up, dressed, and joined the rest of the family as they were packing their belongings into large wicker baskets that would be attached to the donkeys and camels they would be using for their journey. The king had provided them two *harmamaxas* (covered carriages) for the women and children to ride in. The family spent the entire day packing for the long journey ahead.

The sun was once again setting behind the surrounding mountains. Sura and her family were inside their home when they heard a horse quickly approaching. Otanes put on his outer garment and went outside to see who it was.

"May I be of assistance?" Otanes asked as he kept his hand on top of the sword which was on his side.

A rough-looking man with leathery skin and a long beard wiped perspiration from his brow. "Queen Esther has requested a woman by the name of Sura to appear before her."

Sura was right inside the door when she heard her name mentioned. She put her head covering on and stepped outside. "I am Sura. What is this about?"

The man dismounted his horse. He was one of the king's couriers, and his steed was a beautiful black horse with a long, flowing mane. Only the fastest horses were used by the king's couriers. "The queen heard about you and your family leaving Susa and ordered me to summon you. That's all I know." He placed a step on the ground for Sura to mount the horse.

Sura struggled getting on the horse. Her son Otanes helped to lift her up and place her gently on the horse's back.

Sura smiled. "Son, you are so strong. You are just like your father, Farhad."

Otanes had a big grin on his face. He loved being compared to the father he never got to know. He often wondered what his life would have been like if he had grown up having a father.

Sura and the courier made their way through the crowded market place of Susa, beyond the king's garden, and to the palace. Once inside the palace one of the queen's servants brought Sura through very large, brass doors that lead to Queen Esther's bedchamber.

The past forty years had been gracious to the queen. Although she was close to sixty, her skin still glowed with youthfulness. Her blue eyes were still bright; only her graying hair gave away her age.

Sura approached Esther's bedchamber. She could barely make out Queen Esther lying on her couch. "Please pardon me, my queen. My eyesight is failing, and I have difficulty getting around."

The queen dismissed her servant, then stood up, and walked over to Sura. "Here, take my hand, and I'll guide you to a couch. And, please, don't call me queen. I am still just Esther to you, my friend."

Sura sat on the couch and the queen said to her, "I've been informed you and your family will be going with Nehemiah to Jerusalem. You may be gone for many years, so I wanted to see you one more time before your departure."

Sura turned towards the queen. "Many years ago, my dear friend Chista thought your position as queen would change you. She was wrong—very wrong. Once again, you are concerned with someone else's welfare."

The queen reached out and patted Sura's hand. "And you, my dear Sura, are just as sweet as the day I met you."

Esther stood up and walked over to a table that had a large, medium, and small golden box on it. She picked up the large box and took it to Sura.

She handed it to Sura and said, "This is my contribution for the rebuilding of the wall around Jerusalem. King Artaxerxes has given Nehemiah much gold and silver. I would also like to contribute. Remember, these are my people too."

Sura opened the box and even with her poor eyesight she could tell it was full of gold coins. "Esther, this is very generous. I thank you, and so will the people of Jerusalem."

The queen arose and once again went to the table; this time she picked up the small golden box and gave it to Sura. She opened it and asked, "What's this for?"

Esther gave her a big smile, bent down, and hugged her. "This is for your family and your new life in Jerusalem."

The smaller box was also full of gold coins. Sura exclaimed, "This is too much! I can't accept this very generous gift."

Queen Esther patted her hand and told her, "You called it exactly what it is, 'a gift', and what do you do with a gift? You accept it."

The queen got up once again and handed Sura the medium size box. "This is for your granddaughter on her wedding day. I have had it sealed to preserve what is inside. All I ask from you is for you to care for it and not open it until she is to be wed."

Sura got up and bowed before the queen, but Esther gently raised her up. "I'll have none of that. You are no longer my servant; you are my friend. Farewell, my friend, and Godspeed."

"Godspeed to you also, my friend," Sura proclaimed as she wiped a tear away.

After they hugged goodbye, Queen Esther called for her eunuch to help Sura carry the gifts. Sura got to the door and turned to take one more blurry look at the queen. She knew she would never see her again in this life.

∂∾∽

Sura had one more stop to make before leaving Susa. Chista and Sura had remained friends all these years through marriages, births, and the death of Sura's husband. Sura walked toward Chista's modest, little home. She could still imagine Chista when she was young and twirling around in the shawl the king had given her, but the years had taken their toll on Chista. She was no longer youthful looking, nor vibrant.

Sura knocked on Chista's door. One of Chista's grandchildren came running out the door almost knocking her down.

Chista spoke up. "I'm sorry Sura. These grandchildren of mine are very rambunctious, but I love them so." Chista grabbed Sura by the arm, guided her to a chair, and asked her, "What brings you to my home today? Is everything okay?"

"Yes, things are fine, but my family and I are going with the king's cupbearer to help rebuild the wall around Jerusalem. The king is financing the venture, and my family and I may never return to Susa. I could not leave without saying goodbye to my good friend." Sura reached out and grabbed Chista's hands.

Chista laughed. "Not the hands of the young maiden you met so long ago, right?"

Sura also laughed. "Neither of us are spring chickens anymore. We both have gray hair, failing eyesight…"

Chista added, "And don't forget my bent over back. I look like one of those camels my husband rides!"

They both laughed so hard they started crying.

"It's true we are not what we once were, but we are also not what we will be one day. God is not through with us yet, my friend," Sura avowed.

Sura stood up and gave her friend a hug. "Farewell, my dear friend. May the God of heaven and earth shine on you and your family."

Chista hugged her back. "And may your trials be few and your blessings many."

Sura left, knowing she would never forget the years she spent in the queen's service, her friendship with the queen, and, of course, her friendship with Chista.

# TIME TO JOURNEY

# 9

Morning came with the noise of much shuffling around. Sura and her family were busy putting the last of their possessions into the baskets on the camels.

Otanes helped his mother inside her harmamaxa. "Here Maman, you and Shemmah will travel in this one, and Shirin and the boys will travel in the harmamaxa behind yours. Nehemiah and I will be in front of the caravan. The other soldiers and their wives and children will bring up the rear of the caravan."

Sura reached over and picked up the largest of the golden boxes which Queen Esther had given her and handed it to her son. "Otanes give this to Nehemiah. This is from the queen for the rebuilding of the wall."

Otanes opened it up and gasped, "Oh my, this is a very generous gift. Nehemiah will be quite pleased with the amount of supplies this will buy."

At the beginning of their journey to Jerusalem, Shemmah was snuggled in Sura's arms. "Maman-Bozorg, our entire lives we have lived in Susa. Why must we leave everything behind and go to Jerusalem?"

The harmamaxa had lots of cushions inside. Sura leaned back and made herself comfortable. "Shemmah, I know change is difficult, but remember how Queen Esther went from a simple life to queen and how God used her access to the king to save the Jews from annihilation. Her cousin told her that perhaps it was for 'a time like this' that she was in a position as queen so she could save her people. We too have been placed in a position where we can help our people to have a homeland again. It's God's providence, our journey—for a time like this."

After riding for several hours, the sun was high in the sky and was blistering hot. Although the harmamaxa provided protection from the sun, with the curtains down for privacy, it would not allow for the flow of fresh air. Sura tried to lean out the side of the harmamaxa to pull back the curtains, and almost fell out of the opening. Shemmah grabbed hold of her grandmother's waist and pulled her back inside.

Sura fell back, almost landing on Shemmah's lap. "Maman-Bozorg, what are you doing!? You could have been killed!"

Just then, the caravan stopped and Otanes pulled back the curtains to his mother's harmamaxa. "Maman, what happened? I heard a commotion and looked back and saw you half-way hanging out the side. You could have been killed."

Sura sat straight-up on one of the cushions and was arranging her hair back in order. "It was getting too hot and stuffy in here, son. I was just trying to get a little fresh air for Shemmah and me."

Otanes shook his head. "Maman, you are half-blind. Next time you need some fresh air, just ask and I will stop and pull back the curtains for you. I lost my father long ago and I'm not ready to lose you by some silly accident. Next time call on me, all right?"

Sura had a sheepish look on her face. "Yes, son, I will call on you next time."

Sura didn't like being so dependent on her son, but as she was getting older she realized the tables were now turned. It was as if he were now the adult and she as the child. She didn't like being dependent on others for so many things, but she knew it was a reality she was just going to have to accept.

The caravan continued on their journey until it was almost dark and came to a stop at an oasis that had lots of date palms and fresh water for the horses, camels, and oxen. Otanes got off his camel and approached Sura. "Maman, we are stopping here for the night. You, Shirin, and the children need to help make camp."

Shirin, Sura, and the children got out of their harmamaxas. Shirin and Sura collected the pans and cooking utensils they would need to cook their meal. The men slaughtered a lamb and prepared it for their dinner, and the children gathered wood for the fire and dates which had fallen from the date palms.

Shirin and Sura were cooking when Shirin asked, "What will our lives be like in Jerusalem? I have never lived anywhere else other than Susa."

Sura stirred the stew in the pot. "It's difficult for you I'm sure, just as it is difficult for all of us. The unknown is scary, but our God has been for us, and I know he will continue to be for us forever. Just believe."

Though the sun was setting, the temperature had not dropped much. Shirin wiped perspiration from under her dark, brown hairline. "I want to believe, but it is easier for you Jews than us Persians to believe in your God."

"Shirin, all you must do is look at all the times our God has saved us from total annihilation. The feast of Purim is just one example of that, along with how God saved us from Pharaoh and the land of Egypt." Sura reached out and grabbed Shirin's hands in hers and held them to her face. "My sweet Shirin, I have come to love you as my own daughter. I have seen your faith in action many times. Don't let these doubts affect the difference we will all make once we are in Jerusalem. God has a plan for your life, Otanes, the children, and my life too."

Otanes and the children arrived just as the stew finished cooking. Otanes gave thanks for a safe journey thus far and the meal set before them. They still had a long journey ahead of them, so after dinner, the women cleaned everything up and went to bed. The women and children slept in their harmamaxas and the men slept out in the open air.

Shemmah slept with Sura in the harmamaxa. Sura sank into the cushions, adjusting them just right for a good night's sleep. Shemmah spoke in a soft, quiet voice, "Maman-Bozorg, what do you think we will find when we get to Jerusalem? Do you think your father, mother, and brothers are still alive?"

"I don't know what we'll find. It's doubtful my parents are still alive due to the hard life they were living. Perhaps some of my brothers are still in the land of the living; and who knows, I may have sisters-in-law and nephews, and nieces." Sura started tickling Shemmah, and as she squealed Sura asked, "Are you going to ask me anymore questions, or must I continue to tickle you?"

"Okay, I'll be quiet." She sank into the cushions and whispered, "Goodnight Maman-Bozorg."

"Goodnight, my precious Shemmah."

ॐ∙ॐ

The next morning, they arose early and continued their travels. Shemmah and Sura once again rode in the harmamaxa surrounding themselves with lots of cushions. When the temperature would rise, Sura called for Otanes, just as he asked her to, and he lifted the curtains on each side of the harmamaxa to allow for a fresh flow of air.

Each day was without incident until they arrived at the Euphrates River. It was good they were traveling in mid-summer. The Euphrates was at a low water-level that time of year. Nevertheless, it was a slow and bumpy ride through the water to the other side. Otanes guided the oxen through the shallow water, and just as they arrived on the other side of the Euphrates, several governors of the region stopped their caravan.

One of the governors, by the name of Sanballat, asked Nehemiah, "Who gave you permission to travel through our region? Where are you going, and what are you here for?"

Nehemiah approached the two governors, Sanballat and Tobiah. They were in full armor, helmets on their heads, and swords by their sides. Nehemiah answered, "We are heading for Jerusalem to help rebuild the wall around the city. As you can see, we have all of our papers in order, signed and sealed by King Artaxerxes himself."

Both men were furious about Nehemiah and the others helping to rebuild the wall around Jerusalem, for they hated the Jews; but they had little choice other than to let them pass. After all, they had the blessings of the king himself, and they didn't want to provoke the wrath of the king.

# TIME FOR FAMILY

# 10

Afte traveling for two months by caravan, they finally arrived in Jerusalem just as the sun was setting. They rode through the Kidron Valley and through what was left of the eastern gate.

"Oh Shemmah, look at all the destruction. We have much work to do here," Sura groaned.

When the caravan stopped, the men got off their camels, the women and children got out of their harmamaxas, and everyone looked around. Otanes approached Nehemiah, "Sir, what is the plan? Where should we take our families?"

"Since it's almost dark, I suggest we camp here close to the eastern gate. In the morning, we'll explore and meet up with the rulers of Jerusalem and try to find our family tribes."

❧

Morning came, and in the daylight the immense destruction was more than Sura could bear. She wept, wondering if any of her brothers were still alive.

Nehemiah located the local officials and the archives indicating where in or around Jerusalem each of the tribes was living. Otanes read through the documents and saw where their tribe was residing. According to the archives, Sura's family lived outside of the torn down walls of Jerusalem in a small community called Bethany. Otanes, Shirin, Sura, and the children headed out through what was once the Fountain Gate, and traveled for about half an hour before they entered the town of Bethany.

Otanes approached an elderly man with a hunched back in the town square. "We have traveled from Persia with permission from King Artaxerxes, to help rebuild the wall around Jerusalem. We are trying to find family listed in the archives as living here. Do you know where Jonathan, son of Shemaiah lives?"

"Jonathan was a neighbor of mine, but is now deceased. His eldest son, Zechariah, is in charge of the household now. My name is Maai, and I am also of the tribe of Levi. Come follow me, and I will take you to your relatives."

The oxen stopped in front of a mud brick hut, and a tall, gray-haired man came outside to greet them.

Maai spoke up. "Zechariah, these people have traveled from Persia to help rebuild the wall around Jerusalem. They say they are your relatives."

Sura stepped down out of the harmamaxa. Zechariah looked intently into her face and started sobbing, "Can it be? Is this really my sister Sura after all these years?"

"Yes, my brother, it is I, Sura."

They both embraced and then took a long look at each other.

Zechariah looked around at Sura's family and asked, "Who are these you brought with you?"

Each family member stepped forward when Sura introduced them and kissed Zechariah on each cheek. "This is my son Otanes, my daughter-in-law Shirin, my grandsons Babak and Narses, and my granddaughter Shemmah."

Zechariah looked at Shemmah and wiped away tears from the corners of his eyes. "Sura, your granddaughter looks just like you did when you were her age. Abba (Hebrew - Father) and Ima (Hebrew - Mother) were never the same after they sold you into slavery. The years of guilt took their toll on both. Ima died about ten years ago, and Abba died the following year."

Three women and two men came out of the hut. Zechariah stood up straight and proudly announced his family, "This is my wife, Rebekah, our two sons Aaron and Benjamin, and their wives Hannah and Miriam."

The families embraced and kissed each other. Sura looked around and asked Zechariah, "Where are my other two brothers?"

He got a serious look on his face. "Our brother Jacob died while hunting, when he was a lad. Our brother Binu lives next to us with his family right there." He pointed to a home next door to them.

Binu walked out of his hut with his wife, and their family followed right behind them. "Zechariah, who are these people?"

Zechariah grinned from ear to ear. "These people are our family. This is Sura and her family from Persia."

Binu took a step backwards, and after he composed himself, he ran up to Sura and kissed her on her cheeks. "I can't believe it's you after all these years. I was only eleven when you went to Persia, but I never forgot about you." He looked around at Sura's family. "Is this your family?"

With tears of joy streaming down Sura's cheeks, she one by one introduced each member of her family. When she finished, she explained about their traveling with Nehemiah, and about the king financing the rebuilding of the wall.

Binu walked over to his wife Dinah, his son Eli, and Eli's wife Rachel and introduced them to Sura and her family. "And this is Eli's and Rachel's baby daughter, Ruth," he said as he picked her up from her mother's arms.

Binu held her up high and the baby giggled with delight. "She brings us so much joy."

Sura's daughter-in-law Shirin quickly took a liking to the baby girl. "She reminds me of Shemmah just a few years ago." She picked up Ruth's little hand. "My how time passes so quickly."

Zechariah spoke up. "You have traveled far. Please let us prepare a meal and celebrate the reunion of our family. We can all visit with one another while we are breaking bread. Aaron, you and Benjamin go and slaughter two of our lambs. Rebekah, you, Hannah, and Miriam heat up the oven and prepare a feast for our families."

Binu's, Zechariah's, and Sura's families all helped with the preparations. Sura and her brothers went inside Zechariah's home and visited. The home was a modest home made from mud and straw bricks, with stairs on the side of the house which went all the way to the flat roof. The roof was built from sticks, thorn bushes, and mortar.

Sura and her brothers sat across the table from one another in the one room hut. Zechariah grabbed a pot of tea and poured some for his brother and sister. He furrowed his brow and said, "I heard the king was sending Nehemiah here as governor to help in the rebuilding of the wall, but I don't think Nehemiah knows just how dangerous a task this will be. We have many enemies who do not want to see Jerusalem become a vibrant city once more. They want the wall to remain in disrepair, knowing it will keep us vulnerable to their attacks."

A look of concern came across Sura's face. "We have been sent here with a purpose. It is important we don't look at the many obstacles, but look to God for strength. If he is in this rebuilding, which I believe he is, it will happen. We need to be a strong front to our enemies, and be supportive to our leader, Nehemiah."

Binu replied. "You have not been here at our many skirmishes with our enemies. They resent the fact we came back here after our exile with the king's blessing and money to rebuild."

Zechariah nodded his head in agreement. "Sura, what you are saying is commendable, but we are literally surrounded by enemies. The Samarians, the Ammonites, and the Ashdodites, just to name a few. Some have pretended to be our allies, only to prove themselves otherwise. Binu and I are just being realistic. Have you seen the degree of destruction to the wall?"

Sura nodded her head. "I saw only a small portion on our way here this morning. I agree, it is a large undertaking, but the king has sent Nehemiah for a time like this."

Their conversation was waning when their families came inside with baked bread, roasted lamb, and a variety of fruits and vegetables from their garden. They were all enjoying each other's company. There was much joy and laughter as they sat around the table.

Shemmah and her cousin, Jacob, started giggling. Jacob's father, Benjamin asked, "What are the two of you giggling about?"

Jacob was trying to speak, but he kept giggling between words, "Shemmah thought," Jacob laughed, "that our sheep," he laughed again, "are goats."

Shemmah tried to defend herself. "Well, how am I supposed to know? I grew up in the city. Anyway, you," Shemmah laughed, "thought everyone in the city," she laughed again, "was rich."

Everyone at the table started laughing. Through tears of laughter Sura said, "Oh Jacob, if only what you said was true. We would be dressed in beautiful silk garments, not scratchy wool. *Baah-ah-ah.*"

The laughter continued with much joviality until Otanes got up from the table. "I hate to leave such wonderful company, but Nehemiah has requested I help him with something."

Shirin stood up and walked over to her husband. "Do you know what it is you will be doing and how long you will be gone?"

He started putting on his outer garment. "No, he didn't go into detail. I will send word to you as soon as I know." He kissed his wife on her forehead.

Zechariah got up. "Don't worry about your family. You are all part of our family now. Sura, Shirin, and the children will be safe here."

Otanes gave Zechariah a kiss on each cheek. "Bless you, my uncle."

Much needed to be done to prepare sleeping arrangements for Sura and her family. Everyone started unloading the baskets off the camels. Zechariah and Binu placed some of the items into a mud-brick shed between their homes.

Zechariah wiped the sweat from his brow. "I hope this will be okay, until tomorrow. We do have extra mats and cushions for each of you to sleep on."

Sura smiled a little grin. "You have been most gracious. I would like to somehow show my gratitude in some small way. Oh, I know…" She reached for something out of one of the baskets. "Let me play you some songs on my harp. I learned these songs many years ago. Perhaps you are familiar with them."

Sura started playing her harp and singing as Zechariah, Binu, and their families joined in singing at the top of their lungs. Tears formed in Zechariah's eyes and streamed down his face.

"Oh, Sura," Zechariah said between sobs. "You still remember the song we sang when we were just children. So often over the years, I would sing this song and wonder where you were. It is good indeed to have you here." He patted his sister's hand.

Zechariah's son Aaron stood up. "So, Father, this is who you learned this song from. I used to wonder. I would see you were in another world when we would sing this song. Now I understand."

Sura and her brothers were all from the tribe of Levi and were musically trained from their infancy. The Levites were in charge of the temple, the implements of the temple, and leading the Jews in worship through music.

The night progressed, and no one wanted it to be over. What a wonderful night it had been, but try as they might to stay up, they were all yawning and rubbing their eyes.

Sura was the first to speak up, "How wonderful this has been, but this old woman needs to get some sleep. I may even count sheep if I have trouble sleeping...*Baah*..."

Everyone laughed, and then they said their goodnights. Shemmah cuddled with her grandmother on a large mat which was placed on the floor to sleep on and said, "I never thought I would have as much fun as I used to when we lived in Susa. This is better, Maman-Bozorg. We have a bigger family now to share our lives with."

Sura kissed Shemmah on her forehead. "Yes, Shemmah; this is better...much better."

# WORK TIME

# 11

Otanes worked for two days with Nehemiah as they located residences for the soldiers and their families to reside. On their third night in Jerusalem, Nehemiah woke Otanes, as well as the other soldiers he was being housed with, from a deep sleep. "Otanes wake up."

Otanes sat up and yawned. "What is it, sir?"

The soldiers awoke and got up as Nehemiah told them, "I've told no one what was put on my heart to do. I want to examine the entire wall around the city before I meet with the leaders here in Jerusalem. Go with me so we can see the extent of the damage to the wall and the gates."

Otanes and the other soldiers arose and put on their garments and helmets. They each had their swords at their sides for protection should animal or human enemies approach them for harm. They walked beside Nehemiah as he was riding his donkey. They went past the Valley Gate toward the Dragon's Fountain to the Dung Gate. Looking over the walls of Jerusalem, which had been broken through and whose gates had been burned up, they noticed the stones from the wall were scattered all over. Hardly any of the stones were still in place.

Nehemiah could hardly contain his emotions as he dismounted his donkey and looked upon the destruction. "This is worse than I ever imagined."

Otanes nodded his head in agreement. "Yes, and this is just a small portion of the wall. We have much farther to go."

Nehemiah got back on his donkey. "Let's continue so we can finish before daybreak."

They continued on their quest by first crossing to the Fountain Gate and then heading for the King's Pool, but there wasn't enough room for the donkey to pass through. Instead, they went up the valley to continue their inspection of the wall and entered back in through the Valley Gate. As the sun rose, Nehemiah sent Otanes to gather the Jews, priests, nobles, local officials, and anyone else who would be working on the job to a meeting in the city square.

Nehemiah started his presentation of his findings to the people of Jerusalem, "Brethren and friends, last night I made an examination of the extent of damage to the wall and the gates. The wall and gates are in bad disrepair, and without them, we are vulnerable to our enemies. Let's rebuild the wall and gates and not live with this disgrace any longer. God is on our side, and the king has given us money and supplies needed to finish this project. What do you say? Are you with me?"

With one voice the people shouted with excitement, "We're with you! Let's get started!"

Men, women, and children lined up in front of Nehemiah for their supplies for the restoration work. Otanes was traveling back to the town of Bethany to let his family know about their findings when the two governors who had confronted Nehemiah after crossing the Euphrates signaled for him to stop. They also had their Arab friend Geshem with them.

Sanballat pulled back on the reins of his horse and came to a stop. "So, you are heading away from Jerusalem. Proved to be too much work, huh?" Sanballat snickered.

Otanes stopped his horse. "As a matter of fact, I am going to get my family to join the others in Jerusalem for the restoration work. Nehemiah has rallied the entire city to go to work. You may try to stop us, but we are prepared to fight if we need to and finish this work."

Sanballat sneered. "We'll see just how much you are willing to fight for this cause. Come on men, let's go see Nehemiah!"

&#8667;&#8666;

When Otanes arrived at his Uncle Zechariah's home, he was greeted by his wife. "Otanes, it was horrible!"

"What was horrible?"

Shirin was choking back her tears and handed her husband a piece of parchment. "Everyone was asleep last night when someone slaughtered some of Zechariah's goats and left a message written with goat's blood."

Sura, her brothers, and their families came outside. Each of them was visibly distraught about what had happened.

Otanes looked at the writing. "It says, 'Next time it will not be just goats which are dead. Stop this nonsense of helping with the rebuilding, or face the consequences.'"

Binu grabbed the parchment from his nephew's hands. "Sura, what did Zechariah and I try to tell you? We're surrounded by enemies who want all of us Jews out of this land. They will not cease until they have run us all away from here."

Sura looked up to heaven with her arms lifted high. "All I know is we can run and live in fear, or we can trust the God who made heaven and earth to protect us."

Zechariah looked at his sister with amazement. "Where did all your faith come from? You have lived in a pagan land for most of your life."

Sura smiled. "Yes, it is true I lived in the palace, was raised by pagan parents, and lived under the reign of a pagan king. But for many of those years, in the service of Queen Esther, she and I discussed our God, Jehovah. She helped me to recall my training from our parents, when I lived in Jerusalem."

Binu's face turned red with embarrassment. "We should be the ones with strong faith since we grew up here in God's land, yet it took you to show us true faith."

Sura walked over to her brother and kissed his cheeks. "Now is your chance to show strong faith. Are you and Zechariah willing to fight for the rebuilding project?"

Zechariah, Binu, and their families agreed to return with Otanes to join Nehemiah and the thousands of others in the reconstruction work.

When they arrived in Jerusalem, Nehemiah was organizing the project by assigning each section of the wall and gates to different family groups.

Sura and her entire family were standing before Nehemiah to receive their work assignment when Sanballat and his friends arrived.

Sanballat got off his horse, got right in Nehemiah's face, and started ridiculing him. "What do you think you are doing? Do you think you can cross the king?"

Nehemiah shot back, "Cross the king? We not only have the king's blessing, but his money for this project. Besides, the God of heaven will make sure we succeed. Stop interfering with the rebuilding work… or else!"

Sanballat questioned Nehemiah, "Or else what?"

Nehemiah put his face even closer to Sanballat. "You shall see what our God will do to the enemies of his people. Just as he parted the Red Sea for his people to cross and then released the waters to drown the enemies of the Jews, he will destroy you if you interfere with this work of God."

Sanballat huffed and got back onto his horse. He and his friends were riding away when Sanballat turned and called out to Nehemiah. "It's not over yet. Don't think for a minute you have won."

Otanes, Shirin, Sura, and the children picked up some tools from the stockpile and placed them into baskets on the side of their camels and donkeys. Zechariah, Binu, and their families picked up wood for the repair of the gate and brass for the bolts and hinges. They were also supplied with large logs, ropes, and pulleys to lift the stone blocks into place. These they placed into a cart pulled by oxen.

Nehemiah pointed to the east. "I'm assigning your family to the wall by the east gate. There is a vacant residence you may stay in while working on the wall. It's important that everyone work in shifts. Two or more family members may go back to your homes in the daylight hours to gather more food supplies and to feed your flocks. But for the most part, it's important we all stick together because of our enemies' threats."

When Sura and her family arrived at the wall by the east gate, they found the wall too damaged to be mended. Otanes pointed to an area higher up on the slope overlooking the Kidron Valley. "That area just a few feet higher up seems to have a flat, bedrock perfect for the foundation of a new wall. We will curve the wall around until it meets up with the remainder of the wall farther down."

Zechariah and Binu nodded their heads in agreement. Zechariah patted Otanes on the back. "Good thinking. My sons and I will help you with rebuilding this section, and Binu, you and Eli can work close-by on rebuilding the gate."

The evening approached, and Zechariah laid down his tools and wiped his brow. "Binu, Eli, and I need to go back to the homestead early in the morning to feed the livestock, and then we'll return to work on the gate and the wall. We've had a good first day of work. Let's stop for the night and get some rest."

Otanes also laid down his tools. "Maybe I should escort the two of you. It's dangerous out there with all our enemies waiting to pounce like a lion after his prey."

Binu put his hand on Otanes shoulder. "That's kind of you, but we've lived here our whole lives and have grown used to the threats from our enemies. We each have a sword on our sides and are not afraid to use them for our protection."

So the families each gathered their mats and coverings and placed them on the hard dirt floor inside the vacant home located by the east gate. All night long, Sura kept moving, trying to find a comfortable place to lie down. The older she got the more difficult she found it was to sleep through the night. But it was not just the uncomfortable sleeping arrangements which had Sura upset. She sensed danger, the same ominous feeling she had before they left Susa.

৯৵৵

The sun was making its appearance over Mount Moriah when Sura saw her brothers and her nephew preparing to leave. "Zechariah, Binu, and Eli, I think you should reconsider Otanes' offer of his assistance as your army escort. He's been trained in warfare, and I sense danger."

Zechariah placed his hand gently on Sura's cheek. "My dear, sweet Sura, thank you for your concern, but honestly, we will be all right. We'll be back before noon."

After Sura's brothers and her nephew left, Sura's immediate family and her brothers' families arose and grabbed their tools. Each person placed the tools into baskets and put the baskets on their donkeys and camels. The day was still young, and they had a lot of work ahead of them.

Shirin went over to her daughter and handed her a basket. "Here, Shemmah. I'm putting you in charge of gathering enough bread and fruit from our supplies for us to eat while we're working. Place it in this large basket. Babak and Narses, you can help your sister by filling our water pots with enough water for us, our donkeys, camels, and oxen."

Shemmah started rummaging through their supplies, which were in large, clay pots. "Yes, Maman."

Babak and Narses started out the door to get water pots. "Yes, Maman."

Benjamin's wife, Miriam, called out to her son who was following his father out the house, "Jacob, wait! I need you to help Shemmah with gathering the food while we women help the men with the work supplies."

Jacob contorted his face in disapproval. "What? You want me to do women's work? I need to work with the men, right, Abba?"

Benjamin turned around and grabbed hold of his son's arm. "You go over to your ima and apologize. You are still a little boy, not a man. You are to obey your ima and your abba, understand?"

Jacob slowly walked over to his mother with his head hanging down in embarrassment. "Ima, I'm sorry. I did not mean to disrespect you."

Miriam hugged her son. "I love you, son, but the work I'm asking you to do is not unimportant. You and Shemmah are doing a very important job. Without food and water, we wouldn't be able to continue to work on the wall."

# TIME OF TROUBLE

# 12

Zechariah, Binu, and Eli arrived early at their homestead in Bethany. Maai came out of his hut and greeted his neighbors, "Shalom (peace), brothers. I was about to feed my livestock and could have fed yours too. You are doing important work on the rebuilding project."

Zechariah got off his horse. "Shalom, Maai. It's a most gracious offer, but we'll take care of our own livestock. We told our families we would be back by noon to continue the work on the wall."

Binu and Eli went behind their huts to feed the livestock. They were busy gathering grain for the animals. Zechariah was drawing water from the well in the front of their huts. He was pouring water into wooden troughs when he looked up to see Sanballat, Tobiah, and Geshem ride up on their horses. Sanballat swung his sword at the side of Zechariah's head, slicing a small portion off his scalp. Zechariah fell to the ground unconscious. The men continued riding towards the back of the huts, looking for Zechariah's family.

Eli heard the sound of the horses first and pushed his father out of path of the horses. Geshem's horse stomped on Eli, and Tobiah was about to strike Binu with his sword when Maai came out of his hut with his five sons. When Sanballat and his evil cohorts saw each of the men had a sword in one hand and a knife in his belt, they rode away.

Wailing, Binu fell on his son's lifeless body. "No, it can't be. You had your whole life ahead of you. Why, oh God? Why couldn't it have been me?"

Maai tried to pull Binu up on his feet. "Come, Sanballat struck your brother Zechariah with a sword. You can't help your son any longer, but perhaps your brother is still alive."

Maai placed his hand on the shoulder of one of his sons. "Mica, you and your brothers take Eli's body into his hut and prepare spices for his burial."

Mica and his brothers lifted up Eli's body, and Mica answered his father, "Yes, Abba."

Binu and Maai arrived at Zechariah's side just as he was coming to. "Wha—what happened?"

Binu tore a small portion of his garment and placed it on his brother's wound. "A little deeper and you would have been dead. He only took a little of your scalp. After we stop the bleeding, you should be okay."

Zechariah tried to sit up but quickly fell back down. "Where's Eli? Is he okay?"

Binu started sobbing uncontrollably as Maai answered, "He's dead. Geshem's horse ran him down."

Zechariah sat up. "What did we try and tell Sura? We knew our enemies would come out against us with greater diligence as soon as we tried to rebuild the wall. Now look what has happened."

Mica approached Binu. "What do you want to do with your son's body?"

Binu stood up. "Take his body and wrap it in linen with spices. Then place it on a cart. We'll take his body to Jerusalem where our family tomb is. We'll show Nehemiah what our enemies have done."

Maai spoke with Zechariah and Binu, "It would be best for your family to stay in Jerusalem as long as Sanballat and his friends are seeking to harm you. My sons and I will tend to your livestock."

Zechariah, still dizzy from his wound, stumbled over to Maai and gave him a big hug. "Thank you, my dear friend. Perhaps one day I'll find a way to repay you."

Maai and his sons prepared Eli's body for the trip to Jerusalem. Zechariah and Binu gathered as many supplies as they could to take with them. They didn't know how long it would take to finish the reconstruction of the wall.

❧

Sura's brothers and her nephew were three hours late. Her family had been so busy with the construction job she didn't notice they were late the first two hours, but now she and the rest of the family were becoming concerned.

Otanes put down his tools. "I'm going to get some of my fellow soldiers to join me to check on Zechariah, Binu, and Eli. Something's not right."

Sura nodded in agreement. "My sleep was restless last night. I had a feeling deep inside, tragedy was knocking at the door. This was the same feeling I had the night you told Shirin and I we were coming to Jerusalem with Nehemiah to help with the reconstruction."

Otanes was getting on his horse when the family saw in the distance two horses approaching. One was pulling a cart behind it. Otanes got off his horse, and everyone gathered together to see who it was. When the horses finally got near enough, they could see it was Zechariah on one horse, and Binu was on the horse pulling the cart.

Zechariah's wife, Rebekah, and their sons, Aaron and Benjamin, ran up to Zechariah. Rebekah grabbed hold of his garment. "We were getting very worried. Otanes was going to check on you, Binu, and Eli. What happened to your head? And where's Eli?"

Just as the words came out of Rebekah's mouth, Binu's wife Dinah and their daughter-in-law Rachel noticed a body wrapped in cloth in the back of the cart. They both fell to the ground throwing dirt in the air, as was the Jews custom when mourning, and were weeping uncontrollably.

Binu got off his horse and joined his wife and daughter-in-law on the ground, the three of them crying and holding on to one another.

Zechariah got down from his horse and walked over to Sura. "What did I tell you would happen if we helped with this rebuilding? This is exactly what I was afraid would happen. Our enemies do not want us to have a fortified city once more. They want us dead!"

Sura, holding back her tears, took a deep breath. "What you say is true; they do want us dead. But are we just going to roll over for them and not defend our right to be in this land which was promised to our father Abraham thousands of years ago?"

Otanes stood by his mother and put his arm around her. "Maman is right! Our enemies drove us out of this land for many years, but now we have not only the king on our side, but more importantly, we have our God on our side. He will see the project is completed."

With a tear streaked face, Rachel got off the ground and walked over to Otanes. Her voice cracking, she said, "Where was our God when they killed Eli?"

Sura came and put her arm around Rachel. "Many years ago when I lost my husband in battle, I wondered the same thing. Just like you I was young, with a young child to raise by myself. Over the years, I have learned God's ways are not our ways, nor are our thoughts as lofty as God's thoughts. We may not understand now, but one day things will make more sense. You must choose to have faith in God."

Shirin was holding Rachel and Eli's baby. She handed the baby to her mother. "You must be strong now for your daughter Ruth's sake. We are family, and we will be here with you through life's ups and downs."

Binu and Dinah got up off the ground and joined their daughter-in-law. As Dinah picked up the baby, she told Rachel, "Shirin and Sura are both right. We are family, and we must be strong and believe in our God to see us through this. We can't let our enemies defeat us physically or emotionally."

A courier had run into Zechariah and Binu before the two brothers had reached Jerusalem. They told the courier what had happened, and the courier rode in ahead of them and went to Nehemiah to let him know about the attack.

Nehemiah called for a meeting at the town square for every worker to gather. He got up on a platform and spoke, "My fellow countrymen, our enemies are not just sputtering threats. They have carried through with their threats by attacking our brethren in Bethany. I have set up round-the-clock guards at the most vulnerable places of the wall, and I am assigning people by families with their swords, lances, and bows. Each person should stay inside Jerusalem while this work is being done. Don't be afraid of our enemies, but trust in the one who made heaven and earth."

After the speech, everyone went back to working on the wall. From then on, half of the men worked while the other half stood guard with lances, shields, bows and wearing mail armor. Military officers served as backup for everyone who was working on the wall. Each of the workers had a sword strapped to his side, a tool in one hand, and a spear close by. Nehemiah had a trumpeter at his side to sound an alert if attacked. They kept working, from first light until the stars came out. They all slept in their clothes, and each person kept his spear in his hand when getting water. Soon the whole wall was joined together and halfway to its intended height.

When Sanballat and his friends heard that the repairs of the walls of Jerusalem were going so well, they put their heads together and decided to fight against them and create as much trouble as they could.

Sanballat's face was bright red from anger. "They won't know what hit them. Before they know it, we'll be at their throats, killing them right and left. We will put a stop to the work!"

# PROTEST TIME

## 13

Meanwhile, as Sanballat was planning his attack, there was a great protest by the Jewish people against their fellow wealthy Jews. Some had to borrow money to pay the royal tax on their fields and vineyards or mortgage their fields and homes to get enough grain to keep from starving. Some of the Jews were so desperate for food they were selling their daughters into slavery.

Nehemiah was very angry when he heard what was happening. He called a meeting of the nobles and officials and said to them, "We did everything we could to buy back our Jewish brothers who had to sell themselves as slaves to foreigners, and now you're selling these same brother's children into debt slavery. What you're doing is wrong. Don't you care what the nations around here, our enemies, are thinking of you?"

The nobles and officials said nothing. Nehemiah continued, "I have also loaned them money, but I have not gouged them with interest. This taking advantage of your fellow Jews has to stop! Give them back their foreclosed fields, vineyards, and homes right now."

The wealthy Jews shamefully agreed to give it all back and not to make any more demands. When Sura heard what had happened, she went to Nehemiah. "Sir, before we left Susa, Queen Esther gave me a golden box full of gold coins. She gave it for my family to live on, but I've heard of so many of my brethren in need. I want to give it to you to help feed the poor. I don't want to see another child sold into slavery like I was for lack of food."

Nehemiah took the box from Sura's hands. "Bless you, Sura, and your family for your tender heart. The Lord God Almighty will reward you for the love you show to others."

∂◦◦

When the wall was rebuilt, and there were no more breaks in it, though the gates had not yet been installed, Sanballat and Geshem sent a message to Nehemiah: "Come and meet us at Kephirim in the valley of Ono."

Nehemiah knew they were scheming to hurt him, so he sent messengers to tell them: "I'm doing a great work; I can't come down."

On four different occasions, they sent this message and each time Nehemiah gave them the same response. The fifth time, Sanballat sent a letter with this message: "The word among the neighboring nations is that you and your fellow Jews are planning to rebel. That's why you're rebuilding the wall. And it is said that you want to be king. King Artexerxes will be told this. Don't you think we should sit down and talk about this?"

Nehemiah sent back this message: "I don't believe anything you're saying. You're just trying to intimidate us into quitting. God has been on our side, and you just can't stand it."

Then Shemaiah secretly met with Nehemiah. "Let's find safety behind the locked doors of the temple, because your enemies are coming to kill you."

Nehemiah sensed that Sanballat and Tobiah had hired Shemaiah to trick him, so he responded, "I won't do it. I won't use the temple as a hideout."

Despite the many attempts from Sanballat and his friends to stop the reconstruction of the wall and gates, it was finished after only fifty-two days. When all their enemies heard the news, and the surrounding nations saw it, Sanballat and their other enemies totally lost their nerve. They knew it was the Jews God who made the rebuilding of the wall and gates accomplished in such a short period of time.

Nehemiah set security guards in place and appointed Otanes in charge of the citadel. He told him, "Don't open the gates of Jerusalem until the sun is up. Shut and bar the gates while the guards are still on duty. Appoint guards from the citizens of Jerusalem and assign them to posts in front of their own homes."

∂∞∾

After the tragedy of the death of Eli, Sura, her family, and her brothers and their families all moved inside the walls of Jerusalem for their safety. The city was large and spacious, with only a small number of people in it compared to its size.

Sura and her family located an abandoned house next to her brothers and their families. Though the wall and gates were finished, much repair work needed to be done to their new residences. They took turns working on each other's homes until they finally finished and had a celebration dinner. They placed tables butted up to one another until the tables became one large table long enough to accommodate every member of their families, seventeen people in all.

Zechariah stood up with his cup held high. "I want to propose a toast to my family, my brother Binu, my sister Sura, and their families. Without the teamwork of everyone involved, our new homes would not have been completed."

After everyone clanked their cups together, Sura stood up and said, "And I want to propose a toast to our Almighty God. Yes, we did put much work into the restoration of the wall and our homes, but without God's help, we would have failed. And one more thing. Now that my family is living in Jerusalem, we need to start speaking Hebrew."

Shemmah tugged at her grandmother's cloak, "Maman-Bozorg, how do you say grandmother in Hebrew?"

Sura smiled. "It is savta."

Shirin asked, "What about mother?"

Rachel spoke up, "It is ima."

Binu took his granddaughter, Ruth, from Rachel's arms and lifted her over his head. "And grandfather is saba. Isn't that right, my sweet, precious girl?"

Ruth squealed with delight, and everyone laughed.

❧❦

After seven months passed, Nehemiah sent couriers to notify all the families in Jerusalem to register their families at the temple. When the count came in, there were 42,360, which did not include the male and female slaves. They numbered 7,337 after they were counted. Sura and her family were numbered among the 245 male and female singers.

As the people were gathered at the town square, Nehemiah asked the priest, Ezra, to bring the Books of Moses that God had commanded written for Israel. He read it from early dawn until noon. Men had been set in place to explain the reading, and when the people understood, started crying, their hearts burning with regret for the wrongs their ancestors had committed.

Nehemiah called out to the people, "Don't weep and carry on. This day is holy to God. Go home and prepare a feast and share it with those who don't have anything. Don't be sad; instead, feel the joy that God alone can give."

The families did just as Nehemiah told them. The feast lasted seven days with much merry-making. At the end of the feast, Binu stood up and made an announcement to his extended family. With his face beaming, he said, "I'm sure some of you have noticed Rachel has put on some weight since the death of her husband, our dear son Eli. The added weight is not from overeating, rather she is with child. She should give birth in a couple of months."

In unison, everyone gasped and then cheered. Rachel, holding her daughter Ruth, turned to Sura. "You have been so helpful to me through all these difficult months. When I found out I was with child, well, I just couldn't bring myself to share this news with anyone. The pain of losing my husband, and then the realization I would be raising not one, but two children without their father, was more than I could bear. Your steadfast faith has been an inspiration to me. I finally shared my secret with Dinah yesterday."

Dinah laughed. "Yes, she thought I didn't know. But us Jewish mothers, we know – eh?"

Everyone roared in laughter. Sura looked at her sister-in-law Dinah. "Yes, we know when our children or grandchildren are up to something." Sura then turned to Shemmah and asked, "Is there something you want to tell me?"

Shemmah's face turned bright red. "What, Maman-Ba—I mean, Savta?"

"You and Jacob," Sura said and turned to Jacob. His eyes got real big, and his face showed panic. "The two of you have been secretly bringing me flowers. Although my vision is not what it used to be, my nose delighted in the fragrance of the flowers."

The whole family started laughing, except for Jacob's mother, Miriam. "Where did you get these flowers from, Jacob? I thought the rabbits had eaten my flowers. You are in trouble, young man."

Her husband Benjamin came to Jacob's defense. "He meant no harm. He and Shemmah just wanted to bring Sura delight. You can plant more flowers, and Jacob will not pick them –will you, son?" Benjamin shot his son a look of... *you had better not.*

# THE CHANGING TIMES

## 14

Nehemiah sent out notices to all the families in and around Jerusalem that it was time for the dedication of the wall. He tracked down the Levites to lead the whole town with hymns of thanksgiving. Everyone involved in the dedication went through a purification process, and then Nehemiah appointed two large choirs.

As part of the first choir, Sura and her family proceeded on top of the wall to the right toward the Dung Gate. There were singers, musicians who played harps, lutes, cymbals, and the young priests who had trumpets.

The second choir went to the left on top of the wall. Nehemiah and half of the people followed them from the Tower of Furnaces, and stopped at the Prison Gate.

When the choirs were in position on the wall, they joined in unison and sang a song written by King David, long ago. Sura was playing her harp and singing at the top of her lungs. Shemmah was next to her, singing and playing the cymbals. Each member of her family joined in the celebration by singing and playing their instruments.

Sura started crying, and Shemmah asked her, "What's wrong, Savta?"

Sura wiped the tears from her eyes and answered, "These are tears of joy."

Sura's grandsons, Babak and Narses, were right behind the leader of the procession as the two choirs joined together as one huge choir in the temple. The sound of the singers singing made the rafters ring. The sound of jubilation was so loud; it was heard far and wide.

The surrounding nations heard about the dedication of the wall. They were just biding their time for another opportunity to attack Jerusalem.

Shirin and Otanes were close behind Sura, when Shirin looked over at her husband. "I understand now why you Jews love Jerusalem. This is a special place. I can feel the presence of God here."

Otanes smiled a big, wide grin. "Yes, I too feel the presence of God. I never felt it when I lived in Susa. I'm glad the king has allowed me to stay as a guard here in Jerusalem."

෴

A couple of months after the dedication celebration, Zechariah was in the temple courtyard when Binu rode in on his horse. He was very excited. "It's Rachel—she's giving birth! Come on, brother! You are about to be a great-uncle once again!"

When Zechariah and Binu arrived at the house, the women were all gathered together in another room with Rachel. The men and children were in the front room and could hear much shuffling around and then suddenly a loud: *WAAAH—WAAAH—WAAAH*.

Dinah came out of the room where the women had been with a solemn look on her face. Binu was concerned and asked her, "Are Rachel and the baby okay?"

Dinah couldn't contain her happiness any longer. She shouted, "They are more than okay. They are perfect!" A short time later Rebekah walked into the room with the newborn wrapped up in swaddling clothes and asleep in her arms.

Binu walked over to Rebekah and lifted the baby's little fingers. The baby wrapped its fingers around Binu's large finger. "Okay, I can't stand it any longer. Is it a boy or a girl?"

Rebekah asked, "Does it matter if it's a boy or girl?"

Binu held his head down. "It's just—well, I—well…"

Dinah didn't want to keep her husband in suspense any longer. "It's a boy, and he looks just like Eli did when he was a newborn!"

Shemmah had been taking care of Ruth while Rachel was delivering the baby. "Look Ruth, it's your baby brother, your *ach (brother)."*

Ruth tried to say brother in Hebrew, "*AAh*."

Shemmah then tried to teach her the word for sister in Hebrew, "Say *achut*."

Ruth opened her mouth wide. "*AAh-t*."

Everyone in the room laughed, and Ruth clapped her hands and laughed right along with them.

Sura walked over to her granddaughter. "Shemmah, I'm so proud of you. Your Hebrew lessons are coming right along. You soon will be more proficient than I in the Hebrew language."

⬥⬥⬥

Nehemiah went back to Susa to King Artexerxes' service. After Nehemiah was gone for a couple of years, Eliashib, the priest, was put in charge of the storerooms of the temple. He was a friend of Tobiah and made one of the large storerooms available for him to stay in.

In Nehemiah's absence, much corruption was taking place in Jerusalem. The people of Jerusalem quickly forgot the enthusiasm they had at the dedication of the wall and the reading of the Books of Moses. Lead by the example of the priests, they had become complacent. The prophet Malachi was in Jerusalem at that time prophesying against their evils.

The sun was rising above the Mount of Olives and much activity was taking place around the temple courtyard. Malachi stood on a platform in the midst of all the activity and began to address the people of Jerusalem. Sura and her family were also in the courtyard for their time of worship.

Malachi lifted his voice and his hands towards heaven. "Thus says the Lord, the maker of heaven and earth: 'I have loved you, but you have despised me!'"

The people in the courtyard stopped their activities and in unison cried out, "Not so! How have we despised him?"

Malachi looked upon the people. There were men, women, and children in the courtyard, along with animals for sacrifice. Malachi answered, "By your shoddy, sloppy, defiling worship."

The people were agitated. One of the priests came forward and stood in front of Malachi. "What do you mean defiling? What's defiling about our worship?"

Malachi pointed to the various animals. "Look around. You offer worthless animals for sacrifices for worship. Blind, sick, and crippled animals—isn't that defiling? Why don't you priests just shut the Temple doors and lock them, instead of playing religion with this silly, empty-headed worship? There are people all over the world who know how to worship God, who honor him by bringing their best to him. Worship is not important to you. You are bored with it, and with God."

In one accord the people cried out: "You are out of your mind! Get out of here!"

"No, I'm not out of my mind. God has chosen me to deliver this message to his priests here in Jerusalem. If you continue to refuse to honor God, he will depart from you and your children. Priests are to teach the truth of God, and the people look to you for guidance. Yet you have divorced the wife of your youth, and you have married foreign women. The people are following your example. Don't you know the Messiah is to come from the lineage of Abraham, our lineage? You are corrupting our lineage with this behavior. God has said, 'Return to me and I'll return to you.'"

The people moved closer to Malachi and asked, "How do we return?"

"Begin by being honest. You are robbing God by not bringing your full tithes to the Temple treasury so there will be ample provisions in the Temple. And serve God with your whole heart. Don't just go through the motions of ritual."

Sura, Otanes, Shirin, and the children all heard the words of Malachi, and it cut to their hearts. No, they had not divorced and married foreigners, but they had been guilty of not presenting the best of their flock for sacrifice. God had specifically commanded Moses to sacrifice the best of their animals, but Sura and her family had failed to follow the Law of Moses.

Sura and her family began crying. Her brothers and their families, and many others whose hearts were affected by the words of Malachi joined them. Maai was also there with his five sons. They all joined together in prayer and vowed to worship God from that time forward in a way that would honor God.

⊰⊱

Shirin was fitting Shemmah for her wedding dress. Seven years had gone by so quickly. Shemmah was now almost sixteen and was soon marrying Maai's youngest son, Daniel. With tears in her eyes, Shirin stood back and looked at her daughter. Her voice cracked as she said, "I can't believe you are of marrying age. You, my daughter, are both beautiful inside and out."

Sura was now completely blind. She was sitting nearby and held out her hands. "Come closer, dear. Let me feel your face." Shemmah bent down and guided her grandmother's hands to her face. Sura smiled. "Yes, Shirin is right; you are both beautiful inside and out."

In the last few years, both of Sura's brothers had died. Zechariah fell off his horse and hit his head on a rock. He died instantly. Binu, bitten by a poisonous snake, suffered several hours before he died. The younger generations of men were now in charge of the family. Life was difficult for the Levite tribe without enough food to feed their families. The priests were once again not taking in tithes for the Temple treasury, and the Levites were not receiving their provisions.

Shemmah twirled around in her dress. "Do you think Abba will be back in time for the wedding, Ima?"

Shirin nodded her head. "Yes, your father is accompanying Nehemiah from Susa to Jerusalem. They're scheduled to arrive in the next day or two."

Sura reached for a cup on a nearby table. Shirin grabbed the cup and handed it to her. "Thank you, Shirin. It will be good to have Otanes back home again. I'm glad the king gave Nehemiah permission to return to Jerusalem. Without receiving enough provisions for the care of our families, things have gone from bad to worse in the years he's been gone."

Maai walked into the house, almost out of breath. He was a very old man now and had difficulty getting around. "I hope I'm not interrupting anything."

Shirin put her hand on her hip. "Well, since you are not the groom, I guess it's okay for you to see the bride in her dress."

Maai grinned from ear to ear. "What a beautiful wife you will make my son. I only wish his mother was still alive to see this day."

Shemmah held out her hand and patted his. "Daniel told me how she had died in childbirth delivering him. He has told me how much he wishes she was here also."

Maai patted Shemmah's hands. "You remind me a lot of her. All of this is wonderful, but it is not the reason I am here. Where are the men of the family?"

Sura sat straight up. "They left to get food and supplies from the Temple storehouses. Is there a problem?"

"Yes, a big problem." Maai sat down next to Sura. "We have the same problem we had several years ago. As you know, we are not receiving enough from the Temple storehouses to survive on. The priests expect us to do all the work around the Temple and then not get paid. We are starving. If something doesn't change soon, we will have no choice than to return to our farms in Bethany. Some of the Levites have already returned to their farms."

❧

The next morning Sura and her family awoke to a familiar voice.

"Shirin, Babak, Narses, Shemmah, Ima... I'm home!" Otanes threw his outer garment onto a cushion.

Shirin and their family ran to greet Otanes with hugs and kisses. He had been gone for several months on his trip to Susa and back.

Otanes gave his wife a kiss on her forehead. Even after all these years together, she still tingled when he touched her. Sura was the last to arrive at Otanes' side. After a kiss on each cheek and hugs, Sura asked, "Has Nehemiah had a chance to find out what dire straits the Levites are in and the condition of the people?"

Otanes furrowed his brow and said, "When I met up with Nehemiah in Susa I told him some of what was going on here in Jerusalem in his absence. He is probably at the Temple as we speak."

Sura reached out for her son's hand. "Well it's even worse now than when you first left."

Otanes was right. Nehemiah was at the Temple, and when he found out that Eliashib allowed Tobiah access to the storeroom, he was furious.

Nehemiah stormed through the door of the storeroom. Eliashib was sitting with Tobiah at a table; they were drinking some of the ceremonial wine. Nehemiah slapped the cups from their hands and pointed towards the door. "Out of here, both of you! Eliashib, I can't believe you would allow this murderer Tobiah to reside in such a sacred place."

They walked out the door, and Nehemiah started picking up Tobiah's belongings and throwing them out onto the street. Nehemiah then ordered the priests to ceremonially cleanse the room.

Before Nehemiah left the temple area, Zechariah's sons, Aaron, and Benjamin, showed up, and they were visibly upset. Before Nehemiah went back to Susa for a short time, he had made provisions for the Levites to receive regular food allotments because they were in charge of the care of the temple and leading of worship. The

Levites were to continue to receive provisions for their families indefinitely according to the Law of Moses.

Nehemiah walked over to Aaron and placed his hand on his shoulder. "What is it brother—why so gloom?"

Aaron explained, "When you were away, we Levites didn't receive our food provisions you had allotted for us. Living in Jerusalem, we no longer have our livestock and land to provide food for us. Many of the Levites and singers left and went back to their farms. My family has remained, but we were ready to go back to our farm had you not shown up soon."

Nehemiah turned and faced Benjamin. "Tell the courier to send notice to all the officials here in Jerusalem to meet me here at the temple in the morning at dawn."

Benjamin jumped on his horse and answered, "As you say, Governor."

ॐ∘ॐ

The following morning Nehemiah met with the officials in the temple courtyard. He was pacing back in forth, then stopped, and shook his finger at them. "Why has the temple been abandoned in my absence?"

One of the priests started to talk, but Nehemiah shut him down. "I don't want to hear it! I can't trust most of you, except for Maai, Daniel, and Aaron. I am putting the three of them in charge of the storerooms. These men have a reputation for honesty, and I trust them to distribute the rations to their brethren."

Nehemiah continued with his rebuke. "I have also noticed since I've been back, the people are treading wine, bringing in sacks of grain, and loading their donkeys on the Sabbath. And they were buying and selling on the Sabbath. What is wrong with you people? Have you not learned your lesson from our ancestors? God commanded us Jews to not work on the Sabbath. Because of breaking God's commandments, he allowed the Babylonians to capture our city and take us captive for seventy years. Do you want to bring the same condemnation on us once again?"

The people of Jerusalem heeded Nehemiah's words as long as Nehemiah was alive.

# WEDDING TIME

# 15

Daniel was finishing up the addition to his father's house for he and Shemmah to live in. "What do you think, Abba? It looks finished to me."

Maai started laughing. "Eager for the wedding day, son?"

Daniel blushed. "Well, it has been a whole year since I paid her father the purchase price for a bride."

"Yes, son, and you have done an excellent job on the addition. But you know our tradition. The groom's father, that would be me, decides when the groom goes to get his bride."

"Uh, well...what do you say, Abba?"

Maai put his hands on each of Daniel's shoulders and looked him right in the eyes. "I say it's time to get your bride. I'll get your brothers and you go get your friends for our torch-light procession."

Shemmah was getting ready for bed. The last thing she did every night before retiring for the evening was fill her lamp with oil and place it next to her bed.

Shirin had watched her daughter do this ritual for a year now, waiting for the night her groom, along with the best man and his friends to arrive. Then she would be whisked away by the groom into the wedding chamber. "It won't be long now, Shemmah. I have heard the addition onto Maai's home is in the last stages of construction."

Otanes came to his daughter's bedside. "Daniel paid a very large dowry for you, and he has worked hard building your new home. He must have wanted you very much. I believe he will be a good husband to you."

Sura was close-by listening. "Come here, dear."

Shemmah walked over to her grandmother.

Sura held on to Shemmah's hands. "I remember when I married your saba. I was not quite your age, and he was much older than me, just like you and Daniel. Though our years together were cut short by his untimely death, the years we did spend with each other were the happiest years of my life. I pray you and Daniel will come to have that deep love and devotion for one another."

Shemmah kissed her grandmother. "Thank you Savta."

Otanes ran over to the window. "What's all that racket I hear outside?" He opened the shutters to the window and peeked outside. "It's the torch-light procession! Shemmah it's time to light your lamp and get your wedding garments on."

Shirin went to the box that contained Shemmah's wedding garments, as Shemmah lit her lamp. Otanes joined the men outside. The women helped Shemmah with her dress and veil.

Otanes gave Maai a hug and a kiss on each cheek. "Well, it looks like we are family now."

"Yes, and a better family I could never find," Maai remarked.

Thirty minutes passed and Shemmah walked out of her home with her beautiful, white silk wedding dress and veil on. Everyone gasped at the beauty of Shemmah's dress. It was most beautiful with embroidered lilac flowers on it. No one had ever seen anything like it.

Sura spoke up, "Before I left Susa, I was summoned by Queen Esther. She not only gave me gold coins for my family and the rebuilding of the wall here in Jerusalem, but she also gave me the wedding dress she wore when she married King Xerxes. She told me to keep it for my granddaughter's wedding. I have preserved it in this box all these years for my precious Shemmah."

Both the men and the women were carrying their lamps joyfully singing at the top of their lungs. When they arrived at Maai's home, Shemmah and Daniel entered their bridal chamber. The guests entered Maai's portion of the house for the wedding feast. It was customary for the feast to last seven days, after which the bride and groom would come out of their bridal chamber. Maai's sons' wives had prepared a fatted calf, leeks, goat cheese, leavened bread, a large variety of fruit, and wine to drink.

Maai's eldest son, Mica, got up from the table with his cup held high. "I would like to propose a toast to Otanes and his family. We are now one big, happy family."

Otanes stood up. "Thank you, Mica. God has blessed us with many blessings through the years, and I pray we will have many more blessings to come."

Mica remained standing and looked over at Aaron. "Since Eli was Binu's only son, and you being the patriarch of the family after the deaths of Zechariah and Binu, I would like to ask for the hand of Rachel in marriage. You all know I lost my wife and child during childbirth and have remained a widower all these years. I am prepared to provide a generous dowry and will support both Rachel and her children."

Aaron looked over to Rachel. "Does this please you Rachel?"

Rachel looked at Mica and then her cousin, smiled, and answered, "It pleases me very much."

Maai proclaimed, "We've got another wedding to prepare for!"

Everyone cheered.

༈

That week much feasting and frivolity took place. In the evening each person would find a place to sleep and then be back celebrating the next day. At the end of the week the door of the wedding chamber opened. Daniel and the unveiled Shemmah entered to join in with the festivities.

Sura slowly walked towards her granddaughter and groped for her face. Shemmah guided her grandmother's hands to her face. Sura said, "I've lived a good long life, and as I approach the end of my years…" Sura choked back her tears, "I can honestly say I have been blessed. I have been blessed with not only the most honest, hard-working, loving son a mother could ask for, but a granddaughter who has been the most loving granddaughter anyone could ever hope for."

Sura turned towards Shirin. "And thank you, Shirin, for all the care you have shown me. I have loved you as if you were my own daughter."

She reached out her arms. "Babak and Narses, please come here." They both went to their grandmother, one on each side. "You have become handsome young men. Soon you will both be marrying your brides and having families of your own. I am so proud of the strong, Godly men you have become."

Sura addressed everyone around the table. "I don't have many days left on this earth, but the days I do have left will be full of love for every one of you. I can see the hand of God throughout my life. Over and over again, God's providence would happen for a time like this."

Shemmah's eyes filled with tears. "Daniel and I have talked. When we have a daughter, we want to name her after you... Sura. It's a good name, and it would be an honor for our daughter to carry on your name and your legacy."

Sura lived two more years after Shemmah's and Daniel's wedding. The last years of her life were just as she had predicted; full of love. She lived long enough to be there for the birth of Shemmah's first-born child, a daughter named Sura.